The
CHRISTMAS
SHOPPE

The
CHRISTMAS
SHOPPE

MELODY CARLSON

Guideposts
New York

This Guideposts edition is published by special arrangement with Revell, a division of Baker Publishing Group.

© 2011 by Melody Carlson

Published by Revell
a division of Baker Publishing Group
P.O. Box 6287, Grand Rapids, MI 49516-6287
www.revellbooks.com

Printed in the United States of America

Library of Congress Cataloging-in-Publication Data
Carlson, Melody.
    The Christmas shoppe / Melody Carlson.
       p. cm.
    ISBN 978-0-8007-1926-5 (cloth)
    1. Christmas stories. I. Title.
PS3553.A73257C55 2011
813′.54—dc22   2011009648

Cover design: Smartt Guys Design
Cover illustration: Tom Hallman
Author photo: Ruettgers Photography, Bend, Oregon

12 11 10 9 8 7 6 5 4 3 2

No one in Parrish Springs could recall exactly when Matilda Honeycutt came to town. No one seemed to know where she came from either, but most everyone remembered the day Matilda Honeycutt purchased the old Barton Building. Not because she made much noise when her bid won the run-down brick building in the sealed-envelope auction conducted by the city, but because Councilman Snider swore so loudly that patrons in the coffee shop next door to his real estate office actually heard his tantrum.

Word spread quickly about "the interloper who'd snuck into town and practically stolen that property right out from under the noses of the good citizens of Parrish Springs." Experienced in rumor circulation, Councilman George Snider made sure of this. He also requested that the city extend the close of the bidding so that he could have a second chance at securing the Barton Building. "I'll pay 10 percent more than what that woman paid," he promised the new city manager behind closed doors. But as the city manager pointed out, and rightly so, doing this would put the city at serious risk of a lawsuit should Ms. Honeycutt choose to take legal action.

Now, most people would've given up at that point, counted their losses, and just moved on. But not George Snider. Having served as councilman for more than thirty years, he was used to getting his way, and he was not one to back down from a fight, particularly if money or profit was involved. So when he observed the city manager walking down Main Street with that intruder—that blasted Matilda Honeycutt—it took all his self-control not to break into swearing again. Seeing the two of them walking up to the Barton Building, unlocking the front door like they owned the place—when he doubted that the sale even would've been through escrow—was adding insult to injury. Good grief, why not just give that fool-headed Honeycutt woman the blasted keys to the city?

George felt certain this state of affairs would not have occurred back when Leroy Stanton managed their fair city. But Leroy had retired late last spring, and after many interviews and candidates, Susanna Elton was hired to replace him. Her work experience hadn't even been all that impressive—she'd been an assistant to a city manager for less than ten years, although it was a larger town. George suspected the other council members were swayed by her appearance as much as by her fancy college degree. Despite his attempt to warn them of the dangers of youth in positions of power, the upstart got the job. And now this. Leave it to a woman to foul things up royally!

He scowled at the two of them. Susanna, as usual, looked like she planned to be photographed for some highfalutin fashion magazine, whereas that strange Matilda Honeycutt character looked more like a bag lady. What a pair. And what a mess they'd made of things too!

❄ ❄ ❄

It didn't take Susanna Elton long to figure out that Councilman Snider was going to make her life difficult. Although she had to admit that her first impression had been deceiving. Taken in by his easy smile, silver hair, and sparkling blue eyes, she'd let her guard down a bit. But when he called her a "youngster" during her third interview with the city council, she knew exactly where he stood.

"Don't let Councilman Snider get to you," Councilwoman Laxton had told her during a break, when their paths crossed at the sinks in the women's restroom. "George is a card-carrying member of the Good Ol' Boys Club, and trust me, old habits die hard with that man."

"He thinks I'm too young and too female to manage Parrish Springs," Susanna stated as she touched up her lipstick. "That just makes me want to prove him wrong."

Their eyes locked in the mirror above the sinks, and the older woman simply winked as she gave Susanna a slight nod. Then, without saying a word, she dried her hands and left. At the time, Susanna had been unsure as to the meaning of the wink and the nod. But at the end of the day, when she was offered the job of city manager, she understood. When Councilwoman Laxton warmly congratulated her as they were walking to the parking lot, Susanna suspected that the only woman serving on the city council might prove to be an important ally.

At times like now, when Councilman Snider was acting

like a complete jerk, Susanna was tempted to run crying to Councilwoman Laxton. Except that she knew better. Small-town politics were tricky at best. At worst they could derail a career before it ever got fully started. No, Susanna was determined to deal with this herself. If Councilman Snider wanted a fight, she'd give it to him. In a ladylike way, of course. It wouldn't be the first time she'd stood up to a bully.

At least that's what she told herself when she spied him scowling at her and Matilda Honeycutt from across the street. It didn't escape her attention when he ducked into the news-paper office, probably off to one of his Good Ol' Boys Club meetings. Susanna felt confident she could deal with the old coot, but she felt bad for Ms. Honeycutt's sake. It wasn't a very friendly welcome to their town.

"I'm new to town myself," Susanna admitted as she un-locked the door to the Barton Building.

"I thought perhaps you were." Ms. Honeycutt glanced across the street, making Susanna suspect that she'd observed the ill-mannered councilman as well.

"I haven't actually been in this building yet, although I've admired it from the outside. The city I moved from didn't have much in the way of old architecture."

"It does have nice bones, doesn't it?" Ms. Honeycutt smiled up at the brick building. "A good feeling too."

Susanna handed her the key. "Feel free to poke around as long as you like. As soon as your check clears at the bank, we'll get the deed paperwork going."

"Wouldn't you like to see the interior of the building?"

"Sure." Susanna nodded. "I'd love a little tour."

"Hopefully the electricity is on by now." Ms. Honeycutt

flipped the switch, and after some initial blinking, the overhead fluorescent lights came on. "Let there be light!"

"How did you manage to view the property before, without electricity?"

"Your assistant ran over to the hardware store and borrowed a couple of lanterns. We made do."

"That Alice is a resourceful girl." Susanna chuckled as they walked across the dusty floor. It appeared to be hardwood, but it was hard to tell beneath all that grime.

"Yes, she is. Of course, I already knew this was the building for me. Unless we'd discovered something terribly amiss, which I knew would not be the situation, I was certain I wanted this building. Your assistant promised to call the power company and get the electricity turned on as soon as possible."

Susanna ran a finger over a dust-covered shelf. "Looks like you'll have your work cut out for you, Ms. Honeycutt."

"Please, call me Matilda."

"Then you must call me Susanna." She smiled at the older woman. "I would appreciate it if you considered me a friend."

Matilda's brown eyes lit up. "That would be lovely!"

"Do you have any specific plans for the building?" Susanna asked as they inspected a back room with a large door that led out to the alley behind.

"Oh yes. Definitely."

Susanna wanted to ask what but figured Matilda would've been more forthcoming if she'd wanted her to know. Best not to appear overly nosy at this stage. "Well, if you need any help in applying for business permits or whatever, feel free to ask Alice. She knows her way around city hall."

"Thank you, I'll do that." Matilda stopped by the stairs, flicking on another light switch. "Would you like to see the apartment on the second floor?"

"I'd love to."

Soon they were in a spacious room with massive windows that overlooked the street. Like everything else, they were coated in grime. "This could be very nice," Susanna told her, "with some work." She studied the older woman, trying to gauge her age. Her hair was gray, but her face seemed young. "Do you think you'll need someone to help you with it?"

"Yes, I expect I will." Matilda opened a cabinet in the ancient-looking kitchen. "Do you know anyone?"

"Actually, my mother-in-law. She moved to Parrish Springs with me, and she might be interested. She told me she wants to find some work."

Matilda looked curiously at Susanna. "I got the impression you were a single woman."

Susanna nodded. "That's right. I'm divorced."

Matilda seemed somewhat amused. "You're divorced, but your *mother-in-law* lives with you?"

Susanna forced a smile. "I know . . . it's a bit odd. It's partly due to my ten-year-old daughter. My mother-in-law, Rose, couldn't bear the idea of being five hours away from Megan, so she asked if she could relocate here with us. Naturally, I said yes. Rose is such a part of our lives. The property I purchased came complete with a carriage house that someone transformed into a guesthouse, so we even get to have a little space between us. Not that she's intrusive. To be honest, I don't know what I'd do without Rose."

"It sounds like a delightful relationship. I'm sure your

daughter must appreciate having her grandmother so close by."

"She loves it. Megan comes home from school and Rose is doing things like making cookies or planting flowers. She really enriches our lives."

"She's looking for work?"

"Just something part-time. Although I don't personally understand it, she loves to clean. She's the best housekeeper imaginable. I'm always telling her not to clean up after me, yet my house remains spotless."

Matilda blew a dust bunny off the old linoleum countertop. "Well, if you don't think this mess would overwhelm her, I'd love to give your Rose a call."

Susanna pulled out one of her own business cards and wrote Rose's name and cell phone number on the back, then handed it to Matilda. "Here. Honestly, I don't think anything could overwhelm Rose." She glanced at her watch. "Thank you so much for the tour, Matilda. If you'll excuse me, I need to get back to city hall for a lunch meeting with the Beautification Committee."

"You run along, dear. Thank you for your help."

Susanna hoped that it wasn't a mistake recommending Rose for this job. Rose had been complaining that there wasn't enough to keep her busy while Megan was in school. And no one worked harder than Rose. But what Susanna hadn't told Matilda was that Rose had a bit of a Latin temper and could sometimes make life difficult. Susanna was used to it, and she knew when it was time to give her mother-in-law space. But to someone with the gentle sort of spirit that Matilda seemed to have, Rose might prove a handful.

Susanna knew from experience that she couldn't micromanage every potential pitfall. She'd leave Matilda and Rose to sort this thing out for themselves. In fact, the more removed Susanna remained from the situation, the better off they'd all probably be. Besides, with Councilman Snider to deal with, Susanna had enough challenges of her own to keep her occupied. Why go looking for more?

George turned away from the unpleasant scene in front of the Barton Building, but as he ducked into the newspaper office, he could still hear the two chirping females as they went into what should've been his building. He needed to do something and he needed to do it fast. He was ready to implement plan B—bending the ear of Tommy Thompson. After all, Tommy's father, Tom Sr., had once been good friends with George. Tommy had been fresh out of college when he inherited the town's weekly newspaper, the *Parrish Springs Spout*.

As he went inside, the councilman felt almost fatherly toward his old friend's son. He felt certain that Tommy would be happy to get the scoop on such a juicy story, because he knew this was a ripe one.

"How you doing, Helen?" George grinned at the part-time receptionist. He'd known Helen Fremont since childhood. She'd been a few years behind him in school but appeared to be holding up fine for her age. Just fine. In fact, not for the first time, George wondered what was wrong with Rich Fremont for having left this stunning woman. Of course, looks

13

could be deceiving, and he'd heard the rumor that Helen had borrowed money from her elderly mother to get some "work done" recently. George assumed that meant plastic surgery and such, but seeing her today, he figured it must've been well worth the price.

"I'm just fine, Councilman Snider." Helen smiled brightly. "How about you?"

"Well, to be perfectly honest, I've had better days."

She nodded. "I heard about the Barton Building."

He shook his head. "That's why I'm here. I want to talk to Tommy about the whole nasty business. I'm sure there's a story behind it."

"I think Tommy's in his office, unless he's still working on the press. You want me to buzz him for you?"

Her phone began jangling, and he waved his hand at her. "Nah, I'll just go and hunt him down."

She turned to answer the phone, and George headed on back through the dimly lit building. This place hadn't changed much since the days Tom Sr. ran the *Spout*. Back then it seemed much more modern and efficient somehow. Now it just seemed dusty and old. Then again, no one had expected Tommy to stick with the paper this long. Tommy had been one of those kids who thought Parrish Springs was a backwater, one-horse town. He'd made it no secret that he was hankering after those big-city lights. The fact he was still here was a bit of a mystery to George. At least the boy knew how to write a good story, and for a small-town paper, Tommy kept it interesting.

"Hey, Councilman Snider." Tommy emerged from the pressroom.

George greeted him and shook hands. With a serious

expression, he informed Tommy that he was sitting on a real big story. "I think you'll be interested in this one."

"Come on back to my office," Tommy said in a friendly tone. "Can I get you some coffee?"

"Nah, I'm all coffeed up already." As they walked, George filled Tommy in about losing the bid on the Barton Building to Matilda Honeycutt.

"I heard about that," Tommy admitted as he led the way into his cramped and cluttered office. "Too bad for you, Councilman."

"Unless it's not over yet . . ." George closed the door to the office, waiting for Tommy to sit down and get comfortable. "Because I'm telling it to you straight, Tommy, that woman is up to no good."

Tommy listened to the familiar creak of his worn leather chair as he leaned back. Folding his arms across his front, he eyed the councilman carefully, finally deciding to wear his lackadaisical expression. After nearly two decades in the newspaper business, he'd learned a thing or two. In this case, he knew that the less he said, the more he could learn. Councilman Snider was usually long-winded, and if you gave him enough space, he would easily fill it in with words. It would be up to Tommy to separate the fact from the fantasy and decide whether or not it was fit to print.

"What makes you so sure?" Tommy finally asked in a flat tone.

"For starters, this strange broad sneaks into town with no friends, no connections, nothing. She doesn't seem to know a single soul, doesn't even have a residence here—"

"How do you know that?"

"I have my sources." He grinned like that was supposed to be funny. "My housekeeper's sister works at the Golden Door Motel. That's where Matilda Honeycutt's been staying. Not sure how long she's been there, but according to Cathleen, that Matilda Honeycutt is one weird wacko."

"Cathleen?"

"My housekeeper," he answered a bit cantankerously. Like he wanted to know why Tommy wasn't keeping up better.

"Why does your housekeeper think Ms. Honeycutt's a weird wacko?"

"Probably because she is. At least that's what Cathleen's sister says. Now, I'm trying to remember what Cathleen called that woman. Sounded like a bad word at first, but it wasn't. Oh yeah, she told me that Honeycutt lady is a hoarder. You know what that is, Tommy?"

"You mean like a pack rat? Someone who hoards a lot of stuff?"

"I reckon. Anyway, it sounds like she's got a bunch of trash with her. Some of it's in her car. A bunch is in her room. Nothing worth anything, according to Cathleen."

"You mean Cathleen's sister."

"Yes, yes, Cathleen's sister or whomever. Can you imagine why any sane person would haul a lot of garbage around with them? You have to admit it sounds a little crazy."

Tommy shrugged. "Takes all kinds."

"Maybe so . . . but here's another thing. This woman looks about the closest thing to a homeless person I've seen. Yet here she is purchasing a very valuable piece of real estate—getting it for a song too."

Tommy couldn't help but smile. "So does that mean you were going to get it for half a song? Or maybe a chorus or just a ditty?"

"Never mind that." The councilman thumped his forefinger on the one cleared space of Tommy's desk. "Thing is, I *know* this woman's not on the up-and-up. First of all, why's she sneaking around like that? What brought her to Parrish Springs? How did she know about the sealed auction? Why is she staying in a hotel instead of with family or friends? Why does she go around town dressed like a bum? Especially when, according to my sources, she's paying cash."

"What sources would that be?"

"I can't give it all away, son. You're the newspaperman. I expect you to do some of the sniffing around for yourself. Just take my word for it, that woman's got something to hide. The sooner you get to the bottom of it, the better off our town will be."

"Something to hide?" Tommy pressed his lips together and nodded slowly, trying to act like he was taking this all in. In actuality he was thinking about lunch, wondering if today's blue-plate special was a meatball sandwich or mac and cheese. He was hoping for the meatballs, but Belinda at the diner kept switching it around. "What do you think she's up to?"

"Like I already told you—no good! Why, you can tell just by looking at her that she doesn't belong in a town like Parrish Springs."

"How so?"

"For starters, she wears these offbeat, ratty-tatty clothes. Sort of like the hippies used to wear, with beads and strange shawls and these long, weird dresses. Oh yeah, she's got long hair too."

"Long hair?" Tommy suppressed the urge to roll his eyes and laugh. "That's something to get in an uproar about, Councilman. Maybe I should write an op-ed piece about long hair and how you can tell so much about a person just from the length. You think?"

"It's long *gray* hair. Stringy, you know, like a witch." The councilman pointed a crooked forefinger in the air. "That's it! That's exactly what she reminds me of, Tommy— a witch."

Tommy glanced at his desk calendar, which was still open to October. He sighed and flipped the page over. "Halloween was just a few days ago. Maybe Ms. Honeycutt is still in her costume."

"You can joke all you want, Tommy, but I'm telling you there's something weird about this lady. I can feel it in my bones. I've got a good sense about people, and this Matilda Honeycutt, if that *is* her real name, is up to something. Mark my words, boy. She's dangerous."

"So that's all you have?" Tommy asked. "A stranger in weird clothes, a few half-hatched hunches, some innuendo, and small-town suspicion?"

"I'd say that's enough. Besides, you're the newspaperman." The councilman slowly pushed himself to his feet. "You're supposed to be out looking for the news—*you* get the story."

"It seems obvious you're miffed that this woman outbid you for the Barton Building." Tommy stood too, shoving his hands into his jeans pockets. "If she really did get it for a song, why don't you simply offer her a fair price? For all you know, she might be happy to make a few extra bucks and head off on her happy way."

"Hmm . . ." The councilman rubbed his chin as if seriously considering this option. "I suppose I could try to offer her a bit more. If nothing else, it might be interesting to see her reaction."

"By the way, Councilman, I'm curious what you planned to do with the building if you'd gotten it." Tommy walked his visitor through the building toward the front door. "Was it for investment purposes? Or did you have a particular business in mind?"

"I had a prospective client." He coughed then cleared his throat. "Someone who's wanted a prime piece of downtown real estate for quite some time."

"You're not talking about that big chain discount outfit that got turned down by the planning commission for a development over on—"

"Business is business, Tommy. And times are hard. I expect that some folks in town might've appreciated a store where your dollar stretches a ways further."

"Even if that particular discount chain ran some of our respected and longtime businessmen and retailers right into the poorhouse?"

The councilman shrugged as they reached the door. "Whether or not you plan to do any investigative reporting on Ms. Honeycutt, I will continue my pursuit for the truth, Tommy. I will get to the bottom of this."

"If I see there's a real story in it—other than an intro paragraph in *Business Beat*—I'll be sure to cover it. It's not like I'd intentionally overlook an actual news story. Not in a sleepy town like this anyway. Don't you worry." Tommy smiled and clapped him on the shoulder.

"Good to know. I'll be sure to keep you apprised if I learn anything of interest."

"Appreciate it." Tommy watched Councilman Snider's eyes light up as he told Helen goodbye. He wouldn't be surprised if old George was thinking about asking her for a date, but he would be shocked if Helen said yes. Helen was a fairly sensible woman and like an aunt to Tommy. He'd known her all his life and was thankful when she came to work at the paper when his mom got too sick to come in.

Fortunately, the councilman just politely tipped his head to Helen and quietly exited.

"Is George bent out of shape over losing that Barton Building?" Helen asked as they watched the councilman look both ways before he crossed the street.

"Oh yeah. You could say that."

"Are you really going to write a story?"

Tommy chuckled. "There's no story, Helen. Not unless I finally decide to take up fiction. As much as I've always wanted to pen that great American novel, I don't see George Snider as the protagonist type."

She shook her finger at him. "You should write a novel, Tommy. For years I've been telling you that very thing."

"One of these days," he called over his shoulder as he returned to his office. He went inside and just sat there for several minutes. Staring blankly at the clutter on his desk, he wondered what it would feel like to actually attempt a novel. He'd dreamed of it for years, but the tyranny of the urgent always kept him back. Like today. He still had several articles to edit and an editorial to finish, and he hadn't even begun the piece on Coach Harper's last year of football at PSHS.

Just like he did every day, Tommy opened his laptop and told himself it was time to get to work. Although he still doubted there was much of a story regarding this Honeycutt woman, he did make a note to look into it later—after this week's *Spout* went to press tomorrow evening.

He made a note to first verify that the sale was firm and had actually cleared with the city, and then he'd find out what kind of business, if any, this woman planned to open up. If nothing else, he might run a human interest story on her next week—as filler and to appease Councilman Snider. Besides, Tommy actually was curious. What could possibly motivate an outsider to relocate to a hick town like Parrish Springs? And why would an old woman want to buy a decrepit building? He did feel relieved that the councilman had been outbid. It was no secret that this economy had been tough on local businesses. Many were fighting for their lives and livelihoods already, and the cheap goods at a discount chain store would've only made things worse. What had Councilman Snider been thinking about anyway? Probably the almighty dollar—in his own pocket!

To go to the extreme of initiating what sounded a lot like a witch hunt was unsettling. Talking about this poor woman's long gray hair and strange clothes as if Parrish Springs had some sort of enforced dress code ordinance made Tommy's skin crawl.

He shook his head as he opened the *Spout* email account. Maybe the bigger story would be to put the spotlight on Councilman Snider. Except that Tommy had attempted something like that years ago. Naturally, Snider had come out squeaky clean while Tommy was the one left with dirt on his face. Oh, Snider forgave Tommy in time. He may have even forgotten all about it by now. But Tommy still had questions about the old codger. Some people softened with age, but George Snider seemed more hardheaded than ever.

Tommy let out a long sigh. What was it with small towns anyway? They seemed to bring out the worst in some people and the best in others. As for Tommy—well, he just tried to keep his head low and remain neutral. It had never been his plan to stick around this long, and although he felt fairly well trapped by this worthless old newspaper business, he still experienced occasional moments when he entertained daydreams of escaping. Especially this time of year.

He stared at the calendar on his desk. It seemed impossible that it was already November. Next week was Veterans Day, and already he could feel the holidays barreling down the track, straight toward him, like a diesel-snorting locomotive going full speed. Tommy was itching to hop that train. More than anything he wanted to get out of town for good . . . or bad or whatever. Christmastime brought too many sad memories to him. Too much loneliness.

Although Tommy knew forty-two was far too young to turn into an old curmudgeonly bachelor, he felt certain he was on the cusp of doing that very thing.

Susanna checked her BlackBerry as she entered city hall. It was barely noon, and already she had more than a dozen messages that would have to wait until she finished with the Beautification Committee. The topic of today's discussion would be holiday decorations downtown. She was running a couple of minutes late, but these luncheon meetings seldom started or finished on time.

As she entered the meeting room, she was taken aback to see Councilman Snider sitting at the head of the table. Box lunches were just being distributed, and Alice was playing hostess by filling water glasses.

"Glad to see you could make it," Councilman Snider told her in a slightly sharp tone.

"Sorry to be late." She smiled at the small group. "I was just helping our newest member of the community settle into the Barton Building."

"Settle in?" The councilman frowned. "Has it even gone to escrow yet?"

"Ms. Honeycutt made a cash offer. As soon as her check clears at the bank, the property is hers."

"But not until her check clears," he stated. "So why, pray tell, is she taking occupancy now?"

"She's not taking occupancy," Susanna said. "Not that this has anything to do with this meeting—"

"You let her remain in a city-owned building—"

"Ms. Honeycutt is simply doing some planning and measuring, Councilman Snider. She will return the key to my office when she's done." Susanna smiled at Lois Bowers, the head of the committee. "I'm sorry to be wasting so much time on this. Feel free to call this meeting to order if you like." She wanted to ask why Councilman Snider was present. Especially since, despite the always-open invitation to all council members, he'd never attended any Beautification Committee meetings before. She suspected that he'd shown up for one reason only—to get her goat. Well, just let him try.

After Lois called the meeting to order, they began to discuss whether or not their budget was sufficient to purchase some new energy-efficient decorations for the downtown area lampposts. A manufacturer had approached the city, offering them a "steal of a deal" if they could purchase the materials immediately. It seemed another town had backed out on an order, and the company didn't want to sit on them for a year.

"We all know we need to do some upgrading, and as you can see by the copies of the brochure in front of you, these lovely Christmas decorations are top-notch," Lois said. "The question is, can our budget afford them this year?"

"Not *Christmas* decorations," Janice Myers corrected. "*Winter holiday* decorations."

"That holiday still happens to be called *Christmas*," Lois pointed out. And just like that the committee fell into the quagmire that had been disrupting city meetings for several years now—arguing over the separation of church and state. Nativity scenes versus Santa Claus. The usual dividing lines that made so many people act crazy. Susanna had seen it before and wasn't surprised to see it again.

"Might I make a suggestion?" Susanna had to speak loudly to be heard above the fray of voices. "How about if we all agree to disagree on what we call that time of year, but focus instead on deciding whether or not we can afford these new energy-efficient candy-cane lights?"

Back on track, they looked over the numbers and finally determined that the new lights would have to wait until next year.

"That is exactly why I'm here today," Councilman Snider announced.

"Are you going to play Santa Claus and donate the lights?" Lois asked.

He laughed. "Not this time. But I do have a suggestion."

"Please, share," Lois encouraged him.

He launched into a long-winded plan about how it was important to involve the local businesses in covering the expense of making the downtown area more attractive and viable.

"Are you suggesting some kind of fee or business tax?" Lois asked with a creased brow. "Because you know we've tried that before, George. It might've flown back in times of prosperity, but not these days. Money is tight."

"Our businesses are barely staying afloat as it is," someone else chimed in.

"We can't punish them just because it's Christmas," Lois added.

"You mean the *winter holidays*," Janice said. Suddenly they were back at it—Christmas versus winter holidays. Would they never get over it?

"Let's get back to Councilman Snider's suggestion," Susanna interrupted again. She knew a big part of the city manager's role at these meetings was to play referee and peacekeeper.

"Thank you." The councilman looked grateful.

"I have some thoughts," Susanna continued quickly, not allowing him time to push whatever plan he was hatching. "Lois and the others are right. The local businesses can't afford to bear the expenses of the decorations. But I'll bet they'd be willing to participate in a downtown fund-raising event. If we got the chamber involved, we might be able to pull it off without any cost to the city either." She described an event that her previous boss had done to raise money for an urban development project. Just as everyone was getting on board, Councilman Snider decided to play the wet blanket.

"That's all fine and good," he said. "But I don't see why we should let the businesses take a free ride. They need to pay their fair share too." He turned to Susanna. "For instance, the Barton Building."

She felt her eyes narrow at him ever so slightly, hopefully not enough that anyone else would notice. "What about the Barton Building?"

"Well, as you know, it's a real eyesore. Being that it's at the dead center of town, it's detrimental to the entire downtown area. Are you suggesting that everyone else should cover the expenses for it? That smacks of communism to me."

"What expenses?" Susanna asked.

"For bringing it up to standard."

"Up to whose standard?" she persisted.

"Everyone's standard. That run-down building needs a good steam cleaning, the trim needs painting, there should be some flower boxes out front, and—"

"I'm sure in due time these cosmetic needs will be addressed."

"In due time?" He frowned. "Whose doggone due time?"

"In a reasonable amount of time, Councilman Snider. Good grief, you pointed out already that Ms. Honeycutt isn't supposed to take occupancy yet. Do you honestly expect her to whip that building into shape by tomorrow?"

This aroused a few chuckles.

"I'm just saying that perhaps someone from the city would be wise to go and advise Ms. Honeycutt in regard to the expectations of maintaining a property in the downtown area. After all, she is an outsider. It's possible that she is unaware of the standards of, say, the Beautification Committee." He nodded to Lois. "Wouldn't you think it's our duty to inform Ms. Honeycutt that property ownership comes with a price?"

"Well, I suppose she should be aware . . ." Lois glanced at Susanna.

"Perhaps you're suggesting that you, Councilman Snider, should go hand in hand with the welcome wagon, and while they're giving Ms. Honeycutt a gift basket, you could present her with a spreadsheet for what you estimate her maintenance expenses will amount to in the upcoming year?" Susanna said.

There were some snickers.

"It might not be a bad idea to inform future business owners of what's expected of them."

"Which is precisely why we have such things as business permits, Councilman. But that is not what we're here to discuss today." She glanced at the big clock on the back wall. "I have another commitment in less than ten minutes. Could we please stay on task?"

Fortunately that seemed to shut him down. At least for now. She could tell by the reaction of Lois and the other committee members that she'd just gained some of their respect. Even though that was edifying, she suspected that she'd won only the first round in this particular battle. Who knew how many rounds this old guy could go for?

The Veterans Day Parade had always been an important event in Parrish Springs. The tradition began in the 1950s, before Tommy was born. As a child, he'd watched both his grandfather and his father marching in their uniforms. He had always imagined that one day he'd march in the parade too. That, like so many other things, had never happened. By the time he was old enough, Tommy had no interest in going off to war—unless it was to report on it. Being a foreign correspondent had always appealed to him. But over the years, he'd seen enough on the History Channel to know that the old adage was true. War really was hell. That seemed confirmed further when he saw Coral Phillips riding on a float today.

Last summer, he'd included a bit about Coral's return from Afghanistan in his Armed Forces Updates column, saying she'd been injured by a roadside bomb and was receiving medical treatment in Virginia. This was the first time he'd seen her in person. What he saw choked him up so badly he was forced to look away. Coral had been only seventeen when she'd worked as an apprentice for him at the paper. She'd wanted to be a journalist someday, but her family was short on college funds. Even though Tommy offered to help her out in that department, she'd fallen for the old GI Bill lure and shipped off to Afghanistan. Well, maybe Uncle Sam would see to her college education after all. And maybe he could give her some artificial limbs while he was at it.

Just as the high school marching band started playing "You're a Grand Old Flag," Tommy turned away and ducked back into the newspaper office. That was more than enough parade for one day.

Even with the doors closed, he could still feel the thudding beat of the big bass drums reverberating through his chest. He hurried to his office, closed the blinds and the door, put in his earbuds, and cranked his iPod to the Bee Gees. He wasn't proud of the fact that it took these sappy soft rock songs from his childhood to get him through the day sometimes. But it was cheaper than therapy and safer than bungee jumping. He had to get out of this town before it made him crazy . . . or crazier.

Taking a deep breath and humming along to "Staying Alive," Tommy opened his laptop computer and stared blankly at his screen saver, watching the same electronic fish doing the same electronic things . . . for years. He really needed to switch to another screen saver . . . one of these days.

Tommy didn't have any urgent projects to finish—no heavy edits, no fires to put out, nothing was pressing today—but that was expected since the weekly paper had just gone out yesterday. The same paper that was probably lining the bottom of a number of the town's birdcages by now.

He used to obsess over the pathetic waste of perfectly good

trees just to make stupid newspapers. Then he switched to a green paper manufacturer. This company used a combination of poplar trees, grown exclusively for pulp on a tree farm. "Not only are these happy trees beautiful to see from the road, they improve the air quality too," the salesman had assured him. After these happy trees were chopped down and reduced to mulch, they were combined with a variety of other recycled materials and ultimately turned into newsprint, which would end up being recycled all over again. Unless they went on to some other inglorious tasks like wrapping up dead fish, lining pet cages, joining compost piles, or starting cozy evening fires now that the air was getting colder.

Tommy had devoted an entire issue of his paper to living green. He'd even gone as far as to suggest that he might turn the *Spout* into an online paper, but the good people of Parrish Springs kindly told him to forget it. They claimed they liked the feel of a real newspaper in their hands, flipping through the pages with their morning coffee, enjoying the smell of the ink, clipping the retailers' coupons. Besides, as Gladys Lepenstein pointed out, not everyone had access to those fancy-schmancy computers in the first place. So there you go.

Tommy clicked on his notepad (on his fancy-schmancy computer) to see if there was anything there that he'd forgotten or neglected to do. He was reminded that he still hadn't made a point to meet the mysterious Matilda Honeycutt. That was partly due to busyness, partly to procrastination, and partly because he felt sorry for her. The poor woman had been in the Barton Building for only about a week and already she was catching flak. He'd heard her name come up in a number of conversations, and although it was often paired just with natural curiosity, sometimes it was paired with criticism and hostility.

It wasn't hard to imagine where this negative flak was generating from. Not blatantly, of course, but Councilman Snider had numerous friends. Some in high places and some in low. It was Tommy's guess that some of Snider's friends owed him favors. Consequently, there had been three strikingly similar letters to the editor in the past few days, all regarding the city's sale of a particular piece of property and whether or not that sale was handled in a respectable manner.

Tommy had just laughed and placed the letters in his "under consideration" pile, which usually ended up in the trash basket. But it irked him that Councilman Snider was being so underhanded. He was tempted to go over and meet that Matilda Honeycutt in person—and he would welcome her to Parrish Springs. If she struck him as a good person, perhaps he'd even write a friendly article about the town's newest resident, encouraging the good people of Parrish Springs to make her welcome too. After all, if the pen was mightier than the sword, surely it must be mightier than the sharpest tongue as well.

After the parade festivities were over and the town quieted down to its usual subdued self, Tommy told Helen that he was going out. He didn't want to tell her his destination because he'd already heard her making some comments about Ms. Honeycutt too. Not the mean-spirited kind that George Snider was so fond of, but Helen had mentioned the newcomer's strange fashion sense more than once. Maybe it was just a female thing.

Tommy crossed the street and noticed that the windows

looked cleaner and the lights were on inside. He tapped a few times on the door, but no one answered. Since the door was unlocked, he let himself in. "Ms. Honeycutt?" he called. "Hello?"

"What're you doing in here?" a small, dark-eyed woman snapped. She had on blue jeans and a sweatshirt, and her hair was tied back with a bright purple bandana, similar to what his mother used to do with her hair when he was a small boy. But this woman was scowling at him, looking like she might even smack him with the rag mop she was clutching to her chest.

"I'm looking for Ms. Honeycutt. I wanted to—"

"Can't you see we're not open for business yet?"

"Well, yes, but I—"

"And can't you see I'm trying to mop this floor here?"

He looked down at the wet wooden floor. "Oh, no, I didn't—"

"No, I expect you didn't! Look at those dirty footprints you left too."

"I'm sorry. Maybe I should stop by another—"

"Maybe you should just get on your sorry way."

"I'm going." He attempted a smile. "Sorry about—"

"Sorry doesn't cut it, mister."

He just nodded, gingerly backing out the door, but the next thing he knew he bumped into someone, stepping right on their foot. The shriek of a feminine voice confirmed to him that this was just not his day.

"Excuse me!" He stumbled to regain his balance, nearly knocking over the dark-haired girl who was looking at him with a mixture of shock and pain. "I'm so sorry." He knelt down and looked into her face, then peered down at both her feet, which were still intact. "Did I hurt you badly? Anything broken?"

She mustered a smile, and her brown eyes twinkled. "No, I'm okay."

"You're sure?" he asked. "Because I know these big size thirteens could seriously injure someone. I got kicked out of dancing lessons when I was twelve because I stomped on too many little girls' toes."

The girl actually laughed, and he felt better. "Really, I'm okay." She pointed down. "These are pretty sturdy shoes."

"Well, that's a relief."

"Who are you anyway?" She peered curiously at him.

He pointed to the newspaper office across the street and formally introduced himself.

Her dark eyes grew large. "You run the *whole* newspaper?"

He laughed. "Yes, the whole thing."

"Do you ever hire kids?"

"Hire kids?" He frowned, imagining child laborers hidden in some dark attic.

"You know, to deliver your newspapers. My cousin has a paper route in Idaho, and I've always wanted to have one too."

"How old are you?" he asked in a businesslike voice.

She stood up straighter. "Ten and a half."

"I'm sorry, but my paper carriers have to be eleven." He gave her a sympathetic smile.

"My birthday's in April."

"Then you check with me in April." He grinned. "I told you my name. What's yours?"

She frowned. "I'm not really supposed to talk to strangers."

He nodded. "That's sensible. I'm sorry to have initiated a conversation like this, but after trampling you the way I did, it seemed an apology was—"

"Megan," she said quickly.

"What?"

"My name is Megan."

"Oh. Is that your last name?"

She shook her head. "No. It's my first name."

"Pretty name. Pretty girl. And now I will be a gentleman and let you go on your merry way."

"I was just going in there." She jerked her thumb toward the Barton Building.

"In there?" He cocked his head to one side. "You sure about that?"

"Yeah. Why not?"

"I just got thrown out of there."

She peeked through the glass door then laughed. "Abuela threw you out?"

"Abuela?"

"That's Spanish for *grandma*."

"Oh. *That's* your grandma?"

"Yeah. She's working for Matilda."

He considered offering his condolences but thought better of it. "Well, just so you know, she's mopping the floor right now, so you might want to step carefully if you go inside."

Megan laughed. "I'll bet she bit your head off."

He nodded. "Pretty much so."

"Well, if you met Abuela, I guess you're not exactly a stranger." She waved toward a dark-haired woman about

35

a block away from them, walking their way. "And that's my mom."

He studied the woman. Average height, slender, wearing stylish jeans and heeled boots with a bulky cable-knit cardigan. She seemed vaguely familiar, but he couldn't quite place her, although she seemed the kind of person you wouldn't easily forget. He couldn't help but notice that the closer she came, the prettier she appeared. "Hey, is your mom the new city manager?" he asked Megan.

"Yeah. It's a holiday, so she's got the day off. No school today either." Megan jogged toward her mom, grabbed her hand, and pulled her toward Tommy. "I just met the guy who runs the newspaper," she said, "and he's going to give me a job on my next birthday."

"What?" The woman looked suspiciously at him.

"She wants a paper route," he explained. "I told her I can't hire her until she's eleven." He stuck out his hand for Susanna to shake. "I'm Tom Thompson. I accidentally stepped on your daughter's foot while I was making a swift exit from—"

"He was coming out of Matilda's. Abuela had just bit his head off for walking on her clean floor. It's no wonder he smacked into me. I'm pretty sure he was running for his life."

"Oh dear." Megan's mother laughed. "Well, I think our paths have crossed before, but I don't think we've been properly introduced. I'm Susanna Elton, the new city manager."

"Yes, I know I've seen you at some meetings, but I just didn't recognize you in your civilian clothes."

She looked down and grinned. "It's my day off."

"I've been meaning to do a more complete piece on you in

the newspaper," he said, "but . . . well, I guess I just haven't gotten around to it yet. Sorry about that, Ms. Elton."

"Oh, that's okay. And you can call me Susanna. Everyone else does." Her eyes twinkled. "Am I mistaken, or do you go by Tommy rather than Tom?"

He grinned. "That's true. My father was Tom. I got Tommy, and I guess it just stuck."

"I think Tommy is a cool name," Megan chirped.

"Mr. Thompson to you, sweetie," Susanna told her daughter.

"Anyway, I would like to do a piece on you, uh, Susanna. You've actually made history in our town." He turned to Megan. "Did you know that your mother is the first woman to manage the city of Parrish Springs?"

"Really?" Megan looked suitably impressed.

"It's true." He turned back to Susanna, trying to prolong this pleasant conversation and wondering why he hadn't taken the opportunity to get acquainted with her before. Probably just part of his general funk. "Anyway, I really have no good excuse for not doing a piece on you sooner."

"Oh, I'm sure you must be quite busy running a newspaper." She studied him closely.

"So they say." He shrugged. "But being your own boss makes it easy to slack off sometimes."

"And you can't fire yourself," Megan pointed out.

"Sometimes I'd sure like to."

"Speaking of firing someone . . ." Susanna peered through the plate-glass window. "I should apologize for my mother-in-law's ill temper. She's a dear, but she has a rather short fuse."

"Especially when it comes to people messing up her house-work," Megan added.

"She doesn't hold much back." Susanna's brow creased. "I just hope Matilda doesn't mind a little fireworks now and then."

"The good thing about Abuela is that once she's blasted you, she goes right back to normal. Sometimes she even apologizes or bakes cookies."

"I was actually trying to find Ms. Honeycutt," he said. For some reason he was caught off guard by hearing that the ill-tempered woman in the purple bandana was Susanna's mother-in-law. Not because the woman was rude, but because he thought he'd heard that the new city manager was single. It seemed unlikely that a single woman would bring her mother-in-law to a new town. Perhaps he'd heard wrong. For a man expected to be up on the latest news, he was sure behind the times.

"I think Matilda is upstairs," Megan told him. "She's setting up her apartment. It's really cool with all these windows and everything."

"Oh." He reached into his pocket and pulled out a business card. "Perhaps you could give her this for me and ask her to give me a call when she has time."

"Oh, you can go up there and talk to Matilda if you want," Megan assured him.

"But your grandmother's clean floors . . . I don't think I want to upset her a second time."

"It's okay." Susanna gave him a sly smile. "Stick with us and we'll get you safely past the gatekeeper."

Despite his misgivings, Tommy was under their spell, and

he allowed these two dark-eyed females to lead him like a lamb to the slaughter, or perhaps he was headed straight into the lions' den. Well . . . he knew that was a bit melodramatic, not to mention cliché, but it was how he felt as they entered the building.

Susanna was relieved to see that her mother-in-law was no-where in sight as the three of them tiptoed over the still-damp wood floor, then quietly headed for the stairs. "See," she whispered to Tommy, "that wasn't so hard."

"So far so good." His smile looked a little uneasy, but at the same time it almost seemed to brighten the dimly lit stair corridor. Susanna wondered how old he was. For some reason she'd assumed he was a lot older the first time she saw him at the city hall open house last month. She knew he ran the newspaper, but something about his posture or demeanor had made her think he was more like her father's age. Seeing him up close this morning, she thought she must've gotten that wrong. Maybe he really was older but was blessed with one of those timeless sorts of faces, as well as boyish charm. Anyway, she liked him. She could tell Megan did too, and that was surprising. Even more surprising was that, as she knocked on Matilda's door, she was wondering if Tommy Thompson was married. Just the realization that her mind had gone there made her cheeks grow warm.

"Hello, Susanna." Matilda smiled as she opened the door wide. "I thought you might drop by. And Megan too. Delightful." Matilda eyed Tommy. "Who is this handsome stranger you've brought with you?"

"Don't tell me you dragged someone up here." Rose stepped from behind Matilda with a sponge and bucket in hand. "Don't you people care that we have work to do here?" Rose scowled at Tommy. "Not you again!" She let loose a foul word in Spanish and Megan giggled. Susanna glanced at Tommy and hoped he wasn't fluent in Spanish.

"I'm sorry to intrude like this," he said quickly. "If this isn't a good time, I'll just be on my—"

"You got that right." Rose shook her sponge so hard that droplets of water splashed from it. "Unless you're here to roll up your sleeves, you can just be on your way!"

"I could lend a hand," he offered.

"Oh, I'll just bet you could." Rose shook her head.

"Be nice, Abuela," Megan scolded. "This is Tommy Thompson, and he owns the newspaper. If you're mean to him, he might write a bad story about you in his paper."

"No, I wouldn't do that. I just wanted to ask Ms. Honeycutt some questions," Tommy explained, "when she has time."

"Perhaps this isn't the best time," Matilda told him. "We really do have a lot to do in order to open my shop next week."

"So it is a shop?" Tommy asked. "What sort of shop?"

"A Christmas shop." Matilda smiled mysteriously. "Please don't tell anyone about it yet. I want it to be a surprise."

"A Christmas shop will be a wonderful addition to the downtown area," Susanna told her. She could just imagine

41

the spacious room below them filled with all sorts of lovely Christmassy merchandise, artificial trees, strings of lights, plush toys, and the works.

"So that means you'll carry things specifically for Christmas?" Tommy asked. "Like ornaments and such?"

Matilda tilted her head to one side. "I suppose you'll have to wait and see about that, now won't you?"

"That's right," Rose said sharply. "Don't let the door hit you on your way out. And keep your dirty feet off of my wet floor!"

"Rose!" Susanna frowned at her. "Really."

Rose switched over to Spanish, going on and on about how useless men were and how the world would be better off without them and how they were always in the way and taking, taking, taking—never giving back.

Susanna pulled Megan into the apartment. "Help Abuela to tone it down," she whispered. She nudged Tommy out the door and followed him into the corridor, then apologized. Even as she spoke, her mother-in-law's voice could still be heard through the door. "She's not usually that rude," Susanna said. "I hope you can forgive her."

"It's all right," he told her. "I get the sense that she's very protective of you and Megan. Maybe Matilda too."

"That's probably true." Susanna stepped away from the door, trying to distance herself from the tantrum that continued to rage in Matilda's apartment. "I, uh, I hope you don't speak Spanish."

"I took a few years of it."

"Oh." She grimaced. "Did you understand much of that?"

He gave a crooked smile. "Enough to know I should watch my step."

"Well, I apologize for subjecting you to that. I should've known better. Please forgive me."

"Forgiven." He tipped his head politely. "If you'll excuse me, I should be on my way."

She told him goodbye, then opened the door to the apartment and quietly slipped back inside. Rose seemed to have calmed down a little and was now putting her energies to good use as she vigorously scrubbed the windowsill. Her back was to Susanna now, but that wouldn't last long.

It hadn't been Susanna's plan to spend her holiday doing housework. She had simply stopped by because Megan asked to check on things, but Susanna knew if she lingered, she would have the option of either being yelled at or being put to work—or both.

She tiptoed over to where Matilda was showing Megan something in the kitchen, then quietly told her daughter that she was going to leave. "You can come with me or stay here with Abuela," she whispered. "If you stay here, you better plan to work."

Megan's brow creased like she was trying to decide.

"How are your artistic abilities?" Matilda asked Megan.

"Megan is a good artist," Susanna said.

"And with a paintbrush?"

"I love to paint." Megan nodded.

Matilda smiled. "I thought so." She turned back to Susanna. "If it's all right with you, I'd like to hire Megan to do a little painting for me downstairs."

"It's fine with me," Susanna assured her. "If Megan is interested."

"Absolutely." Megan beamed. Susanna wasn't sure if she

43

was excited about the prospects of painting or earning money. Maybe it was both.

"Great." Susanna pushed a strand of overgrown bangs away from Megan's face. "Try not to get too messy. Those aren't exactly painting clothes."

"Oh, I'll give her something to wear," Matilda assured her.

"Fine. I'll be in town doing a couple errands, but I have my cell phone. Then I'll be at home if you get done and need a ride."

"Or I can ride with Abuela."

Susanna glanced nervously to where Rose was now eyeing her, almost as if she were ready to let loose with another tongue lashing. "I better scoot."

"That's right," Rose said. "If you're not here to work, you're not here at all."

"Have fun," Susanna called as she hurried out. As she went down the stairwell, she felt relieved to escape but also a little disappointed to be without Megan's company. She had really hoped they'd have a mother-daughter day, but Megan had seemed so happy to stay and help. Why spoil her fun?

Downstairs, Susanna noticed that the lights were on in the back room. Being frugal by nature, she went to turn them off, but when she saw a lot of boxes stacked back there, curiosity got the best of her. Was this some of the Christmas merchandise for the shop? She peeked inside a box that was open and was surprised to see what looked like the remainders of a garage sale carelessly heaped together. She'd heard the strange rumors that Matilda had all kinds of junk hoarded in her car and hotel room, but she hadn't taken them too seriously.

Susanna peeked in another open box. Same thing. Dusty, old, useless-looking items.

Certainly this wasn't what Matilda intended to sell in her shop. If so, what about the city's business ordinances? A special permit was required to open a secondhand store in Parrish Springs. What would Councilman Snider say and do if it turned out that Matilda Honeycutt planned to open a shoddy little thrift store in the middle of downtown? One thing for sure—he'd probably blame Susanna. But if it was a secondhand store, why would Matilda claim it was a Christmas shop? Susanna hadn't seen a single Christmas item in either of the boxes.

It wasn't that Susanna was opposed to thrift stores in general, she just hated to see Matilda getting into hot water over a permit and zoning issue. She was tempted to head over to city hall, do some research, and see if there was an easy way to smooth this thing over for Matilda. Check into a special permit. A temporary exception. Although she wasn't even sure Matilda truly planned to open a secondhand store. Susanna hated to jump the gun on that. It would be embarrassing to get the permit process going and discover that Matilda was actually opening a Christmas shop.

Susanna remembered there would be no one at city hall today anyway. The place would be locked up. Even though Susanna had a set of keys and could get into her own office during off hours, it would require the use of the security code, and the last time she'd attempted that—on the Sunday after her first week on the job—she'd managed to get the police and fire departments into an uproar. What a way to meet the locals! The incident later appeared in the Police Reports section of the newspaper as a tongue-in-cheek account of the new city manager waking up Parrish Springs early on Sunday morning. She wondered if Tommy wrote the Police Reports section. It was usually quite witty and sometimes laugh-out-loud funny.

No, she decided as she finally turned off the lights in the back room, she was going to stick with her plan—this was supposed to be her holiday! With or without Megan, she planned to enjoy this time off.

Carefully crossing the freshly scrubbed floor, which was almost dry, Susanna let herself out of the building. Unsure of what to do next, she stood for a long moment, gazing up and down Main Street as if she expected one of the businesses to lure her in. Finally she looked across the street to the newspaper office. Tommy had seemed quite eager to do an interview with her, but would it be pushy to go over there uninvited and expect him to make time for her? Probably so. It might also seem a bit desperate, like she was pursuing him. And since when did Susanna Elton pursue men? If anything, she was usually holding them back at arm's length. Plus, for all she knew, Tommy Thompson was happily married with four kids and a dog at home.

Putting him out of her mind, she stopped by Cards-n-Stuff and browsed a bit. Next she popped into the florist shop and bought a mixed bouquet of fall-colored flowers. Rose thought purchased blooms were a waste of money, but Susanna liked supporting the local businesses. Then she stopped by the Shoe Inn to see if the Cole Haan pumps she'd ordered two weeks ago were in yet.

"I'm so glad you stopped in," Lauren exclaimed. Lauren

owned the store and made customer service her top priority. "They arrived with the late UPS yesterday. I left a message at your office, but I suspected you'd already gone home."

Susanna tried on the pumps, which were gorgeous, and walked around the shop to make sure they were as comfortable as they were attractive. "I love them," she finally proclaimed.

"They look stunning on you." Lauren smiled.

As Susanna was paying for them, Lauren asked about the new business in the Barton Building. "It's not shoes, is it?"

"No, I don't think so." Susanna put her debit card back in her wallet.

"Do you know what it is?"

Susanna wasn't sure what to say. Proclaiming it a Christmas shop might be premature. Especially after seeing those boxes of junk in the back room.

"Would you even say if you knew?" Lauren's brows lifted.

"I think Matilda is trying to keep it under wraps for now. Maybe she'll have a grand opening when the time comes. One thing I can assure you is that she is hard at work on it. I know she wants the shop opened up in time for Christmas traffic."

"Cindy at the Clothes Horse is worried it's going to be another clothing store. We really don't need another one, you know."

"I don't think Cindy needs to be worried either."

Lauren grinned as she handed Susanna the receipt. "Judging by Matilda Honeycutt's interesting wardrobe, I think you're probably right." She chuckled. "The Cut-n-Curl probably doesn't need to be too concerned either."

Susanna smiled politely. "No, I expect not."

"Sorry," Lauren said. "I didn't mean to sound so catty. You should hear the talk around town."

"I do hear it," Susanna said. "Bits and pieces anyway. Maybe I'm just not used to small towns yet, but some of it seems a little mean-spirited to me. Matilda is a very sweet person."

Lauren leaned forward, lowering her voice since another customer was just coming in. "How well do you really know her?"

Susanna considered this. "Not that well, I suppose, but I do like her. My mother-in-law is working for her."

"*That's* your mother-in-law?"

Susanna tried not to look too alarmed. "Rose Elton is my mother-in-law. Have you met her?"

"In a way." Lauren looked uncomfortable.

"Rose has a bit of a temper."

"A bit." Lauren put the shoe box in a bag.

"Did you have a run-in with her already?"

Lauren smiled stiffly. "Actually, my husband did." She quietly told Susanna about how Rose had come in a couple days ago. "She wanted a cheap pair of shoes, you know, to work in and get dirty and toss out." Lauren glanced around to see if anyone was listening. "Well, you know we don't carry that sort of thing in here. Larry tried to explain that to her and—oh my. Do you want to hear more?"

"That's okay," Susanna said quickly. "I can imagine. My mother-in-law can be very opinionated about what she considers overpriced merchandise."

"Yes. So it seems."

Susanna reached across the counter and patted Lauren's

hand, looking directly into her eyes. "Please accept my apologies on her behalf."

"Of course!" Lauren smiled brightly. "No one expects you to control your mother-in-law." She laughed. "Good grief, you should meet mine someday."

Susanna smiled and thanked her as she took her bag. Trying not to look like she was in a rush, she pretended to browse a bit as she casually left the shoe store. But the truth was she wanted to tuck her head and run.

Once she was in her car, she took a deep breath and just shook her head. As if managing the complexities of a small town like Parrish Springs wasn't enough of a challenge, doing damage control on Rose was going to push her to the limit.

6

Helen Fremont checked her image in the mirror as she dried her hands on a paper towel. Patting her perfectly styled hair with satisfaction, she knew the hairdresser had been absolutely right. Softening her hair color into a nice strawberry blonde did make her look younger, and the color hid the gray roots better too. Her visit to the day spa over in Greenburg while she'd been on vacation hadn't hurt either. It had been her sixty-fifth birthday present to herself and well worth the expense.

Oh, she knew some folks in town thought she'd gone under the knife while on vacation last month, but that didn't trouble her. Helen had been born and raised in Parrish Springs. Accustomed to small-town talk, she rarely attempted to set gossipers straight one way or another when it came to her personal life. She figured that it was when people *quit* talking about her that she should be concerned.

Helen retouched her lipstick, smiled to check her teeth for any stray spinach left over from today's salad at Zephyr's, then nodded in satisfaction. Yes, let them talk about her nips and tucks if it made them feel better about themselves. Thanks to a lot of spandex and a bit of Botox, Helen Fremont didn't look half bad for her age.

She wiped down the countertop and straightened the mirror above the sink. Satisfied all was in apple-pie order, she turned off the light and returned to her desk. The newspaper office was quiet as a morgue. Thursdays were always slow at the paper, but being that today was a holiday, it was dead. Most of the time Helen didn't even come in on Thursdays. But after watching the parade then having lunch with Violet, she'd decided to stay in town for a bit and put this quiet afternoon to good use. Without the interruption of the phone or people stopping in, she could clean out her desk as well as some old and overly crowded file drawers.

She'd spotted Tommy across the street earlier, talking to the new city manager and a young girl. Then they'd all entered the Barton Building together. Curious as to what that was all about, Helen figured she'd find out sooner or later. She expected Tommy to return at any moment since he'd left the lights on in his office and the front door unlocked. In the meantime, she was enjoying the freedom of emptying out drawers and making a temporary mess in order to gain some order and fresh storage space.

She'd been meaning to do this much-needed task for ages, ever since she'd taken over for Tommy's mother more than a dozen years ago. Being tidy by nature, Helen abhorred the idea of making the reception area look like a yard sale, if anyone was around to see it. She took pride in making the newspaper office—at least the entrance—attractive and appealing. What happened once you got past her end of the building was Tommy's problem.

From her own pocketbook, Helen had gotten sepia-toned reprints of historic photos beautifully matted and framed. Some were related to the paper and some were just highlights of town, but they were hung evenly along the big wall by the front entrance, and newcomers always seemed to enjoy them. She'd scrounged to find a nice leather couch, side table, and brass lamp to put on the other wall and added an old oriental rug from her own attic. She felt these efforts gave what had once been an eyesore entrance a feeling of a somewhat elegant lobby. For that reason, she'd been reluctant to tear things up like she was doing today.

She lugged a heavy stack of faded manila file folders over to the couch and dropped them with a splat. The whole lot of them probably belonged in the dumpster, and that's likely where they'd end up. Just to be sure, she wanted to skim through them first. Out of respect for her old friend.

Betty, bless her heart, saved everything in hard copies and duplicates. Never comfortable with computers, Tommy's mother had been certain that anything stored electronically would one day disappear into cyberspace. Or worse yet, her old PC would be sabotaged by a crazed hacker, determined to undermine the *Spout*. Then where would they be? There had been times, like when their whole system crashed a couple years ago, that Helen thought perhaps her old friend had been right. Then a computer expert had arrived, and like Superman—although he looked more like Clark Kent—he'd miraculously retrieved the lost files, fixed their system, and restored all back to electronic bliss and order.

Helen pulled a fat old file from the mess she'd created on the couch. Blowing the dust from the top, she saw that the neatly typed label on the tab proclaimed "Past Due." Inside were yellowed copies of letters that had been sent to their advertising customers for overdue bills. The top letter, to the Clothes Horse, was dated January 15, 1995. It figured that Cindy had been late on her payment back when that store first opened up. She was still late now. For some reason that date stopped Helen. She thought hard and realized that must've been shortly after Betty's diagnosis.

Out of curiosity, Helen scanned the letter and couldn't help but smile at the tone of the scolding. Obviously Betty had been thinking about things other than late payments. The second paragraph really grabbed her.

> *You are young and your business is new, and you think you have all the time in the world to catch up with these things, Cindy, but the next thing you know it's too late. I encourage you to keep the slate clean. If you owe a debt, pay it. If you owe an apology, say it. Do not leave anything undone!*

Helen felt a lump in her throat as she laid this letter back with the others. Too bad Cindy hadn't heeded Betty's counsel. At least Betty had taken her own advice. She used the last year of her life to tie up loose ends. Why, she'd even done her Christmas shopping the summer before her death. Knowing full well that she would probably be gone by the holidays, she had carefully picked out and wrapped the presents and stacked them in her hall closet. She'd died just days before Christmas. Poor Tommy didn't even find the festive packages until the following summer after he'd decided to rent out his condo unit and move back into his parents' old home. Helen still remembered how he'd come into work that day with a sad smile, pretending to be Santa as he disbursed Betty's gifts in the midst of summer. Christmas in July.

"Excuse me."

Helen looked up from Betty's old letters with misty eyes. A young man, or young by her standards, peered down at her. Caught off guard, she blinked at him. "I'm sorry. We're not really open today."

"I didn't figure you'd be open, but then I saw the lights on. And the door's not locked."

She set the folders down and brushed the dust from her hands as she stood. "It's a small town. A lot of people don't lock doors."

He smiled. "Charming."

"So . . . what can I do for you?"

"I'm looking for Tom Thompson."

"Oh." She nodded. "Are you a personal friend? Or did you have an appointment?"

"Not exactly. I mean, Tom and I met at a seminar about a year ago. He mentioned then that he wanted to sell the newspaper."

"Sell the newspaper?" Helen was shocked, but as usual in a dicey situation, she put on her poker face.

"Yes. He said he hadn't done anything official, although, like I said, that was a year ago. Anyway, I told him I might be interested, so he gave me his card. He told me to call him if I ever got serious."

"I see." She nodded. "And now you are serious?"

"If the price is right I am."

She stuck out her hand. "I'm Helen Fremont. I work for Tommy, but I'm also an old friend of the family."

"Nice to meet you. I'm Garth Price. I was actually passing through town and thought I'd stop and chat with Tom."

"Passing through?" She frowned—or attempted to, which was not possible thanks to her recent Botox shots. Didn't this upstart know that Parrish Springs was not on the way to much of anywhere?

He gave a half smile. "Okay, it was a little out of my way."

"Well, Tommy was in here a bit earlier," she told him. "Let me try his cell phone." As usual, his cell phone went straight to voice mail. Sometimes she wondered why he even bothered to carry it with him at all. He would always say the phone was for him to call others, not for others to call him, and then she would remind him that he was a newspaperman and was expected to be available when a big story broke. Of course, he would just laugh at that.

"If you want to wait, I think I might be able to find him," she told Garth.

"Sure. That's fine."

"Have a seat," she said. "Or, if you want, feel free to look around." She wanted to add, "Perhaps you'll see just how lackluster and run-down this place is and decide you don't want it," but that didn't seem very professional.

"Really? You don't mind if I wander a bit? Not worried I'll make off with something valuable?"

"Like I said, we're a small town. We tend to trust people around here." She cocked her head slightly to one side. "I'll only be across the street, so don't get any ideas." She smiled sweetly and let herself out, then hurried across the street and knocked on the door. After a couple minutes, a pretty young girl answered. Her dark hair was tied back in a ponytail, and she had a small paintbrush in her hand.

"Excuse me," Helen said. "I'm looking for Tommy Thompson. I think I saw him come inside here awhile ago."

"Are you his mother?"

Helen laughed. "Not exactly. But sometimes it feels like it."

"Tommy left." She glanced over her shoulder. "Do you remember how long ago it was when Tommy left?"

The mysterious gray-haired woman came over. Her hair was pulled back in a braid, and instead of her usual long dress, she had on overalls and a tie-dyed shirt and her feet were bare. She too had a paintbrush in hand. "Please come in," she said.

"You must be Matilda Honeycutt." Helen smiled and held out her hand. "I'm Helen Fremont."

"Yes, I'm Matilda." She looked down at her paint-smeared hand. "I don't want to get paint on you."

"No, of course not." Helen lowered her hand. "I work at the newspaper across the street, the *Parrish Springs Spout*."

"With Tommy," the girl said.

"Do you happen to know where Tommy went?" Helen asked. She was beginning to think this was a waste of time, but she was curious. This was her first encounter with the mystery woman. She glanced over to where a ladder was set up, trying to see what it was they were painting on the walls. It looked like letters or words.

"I have no idea where Tommy is, but it's a pleasure to meet you," Matilda told her. "I do hope you'll come back again when I officially open up my shop."

"What kind of shop will it be?" Helen asked.

"It's a secret," the girl said quickly. "No one is supposed to know until opening day."

"I don't expect you'll be wanting to run an advertisement in the paper then," Helen said.

"No, I don't think so."

"Tommy said he's going to write an article about her," the girl said. "That's probably as good as an ad."

Helen smiled at her. "You're right. May I ask who you are?"

"I'm Megan Elton," the girl told her. "My mom's the new city manager."

"Aha." Helen nodded. "I thought I'd seen her down here today too."

"What is going on here?" a small, wiry, dark-haired woman demanded. "I thought we were all supposed to be working."

"That's my grandmother," Megan said quietly. "She can be a little grouchy."

"We're going back to work," Matilda called out.

"There's still a lot to do if you want to open next week," the other woman snapped.

"I'll get out of your hair," Helen said as she backed toward the door.

"Unless you want to scrub down the bathroom," the woman called.

Helen laughed. "No thank you."

Megan looked apologetic. "Nice to meet you," she called out. "Hope you find Tommy. Tell him I said hi."

Helen waved. "Will do."

As she waited to cross the street, she tried to make sense of what she'd just seen. The girl was adorable, but that grandmother, well, she was a little scary. And Matilda was hard to read. Polite enough, but something seemed a little strange about her. And those bare feet. Who went shoeless this time of year? Very weird indeed. No wonder people were gossiping.

As she opened the door to the newspaper office, she wondered what they had been painting on the walls. She suspected the letters would eventually comprise words, but they had made no sense to her. Perhaps a different language. For the life of her, Helen couldn't begin to guess what kind of business that place was going to be, but she'd definitely gotten a weird feeling in there.

As she returned to her desk, Helen remembered a friend she'd had in the sixties, a real hippie who had gone braless, smoked marijuana—the works. She wasn't sure what had become of Sylvia, but she'd heard she and her man had joined a commune that eventually got in trouble for selling illegal drugs. Something about Matilda reminded Helen of Sylvia, and suddenly she wondered if Matilda planned to do some kind of illegal business in town. Surely the city manager wouldn't allow her child to help out someone like that.

"Did you have any luck?"

Helen jumped, knocking a stack of files to the floor. "What?" She stared at the young man. "Oh my, I completely forgot about you."

"Sorry to startle you. I assume you didn't find Tom then?"

"No." Helen shook her head. She couldn't believe that she'd totally blanked out on the reason she'd gone across the street. At this stage of the game, she couldn't blame it on a menopause moment. Maybe she was just losing it.

"Well, I've got to be on my way. I'll give Tom a call in the morning and then try to make it back here for the weekend."

Helen nodded. "That's a good idea."

As he was leaving, she knew she should offer to make an appointment for him, or perhaps give him Tommy's phone number or take his so that Tommy could call him. But the fact that he'd startled her like that, causing the files to fly all over the place, and then he didn't even offer to help pick them up, seriously irked her. That was no gentleman!

She had just gathered the files into her arms and was about to drop the mess into a cardboard box when Tommy walked in. "What's going on in here?" he asked. "Was there a natural disaster while I was gone? Earthquake, tornado, tsunami?"

"Very funny." She stood and brushed the dust from her hands. "For all you'd know, there might've been."

He looked surprised. "What's that supposed to mean?"

"It means how can you call yourself a reporter and run around town with your phone turned off?"

"That again?" He picked up a few of the folders she'd missed and handed them to her. "You know how I feel about cell phones. Especially in restaurants, which is where I happened to be, having a late lunch."

"How am I supposed to reach you if there's a real emergency?"

"If there were a fire or wreck or any life-threatening thing, you know I'd hear the sirens, Helen. And I'd call you for a heads-up. Besides that, Barry is always listening to his short-wave radio. You know he never misses a photo op, and if you don't find me, he does."

"I know, I know."

"Really, Helen, what's troubling you?" He frowned at the debris all over. "And why are you making such a mess?"

She quickly explained her cleanup plan, then moved on to his unexpected guest, who was gone now but planned to come back on Saturday. "I felt a little blindsided, Tommy." She held up her hands, which were looking pretty grimy from the files. "If you planned to sell this place, I'd think you'd have told me. Don't I deserve to know?"

He ran his fingers through his hair and sighed. "That's not how it was, Helen."

"How was it then?"

"I'm sure I was just talking, saying how I was done with the newspaper business. You know how I can be. Sometimes I just need to blow off steam. To be honest, I don't even remember the conversation."

"Well, Garth Price remembered." She was actually surprised that she could recall his name. "He seemed quite interested."

Tommy rubbed his chin. "Hmmm."

"You really would consider selling the *Spout*?"

"I don't know . . . probably not." He gave a mischievous grin that reminded her of when he was a little boy. "But it wouldn't hurt to hear what old Garth's got to say, would it?"

Helen wanted to smack him on the back of the head. Instead she just said, "Humph!" and turned back to her cleanup project.

"Want any help with this?" he asked.

Her first response was to say, "No thank you" in a very frosty tone. On second thought, she wanted to make it home before dark tonight. So, acting like an angry army sergeant, she told him that she did in fact want some help. She barked orders at him, keeping him running back and forth from her desk to the dumpster. By the time they finished, just before six, she had forgiven him and was almost over her bad mood. Almost.

Despite its slightly worn and faded Christmas decorations on the lampposts, the city of Parrish Springs looked bright and festive the week before Thanksgiving. Shop owners seemed to be pulling out all the stops in their efforts to loosen the purse strings of the previously frugal holiday shoppers this year. Garlands of lights were strung, windows were trimmed, Christmas music was playing. Stark's Drugstore was already bragging that, following the Christmas parade, Santa would be spending his entire afternoon on their premises, taking photos with kiddies and handing out candy canes.

Enthusiasm was high, and for the most part, this year was stacking up to be a profitable one for the local merchants. However, there was one small fly in the holiday eggnog. Or perhaps it was a big one. The Barton Building, which everyone had been anxiously watching, eagerly awaiting, and curiously speculating on, looked more dismal than ever. At least on the outside. To be fair, no one could see what was actually going on inside. Not since the big windows had been covered with a mishmash of newspaper, cardboard, and butcher paper.

Thanks to those carelessly blocked-out windows, the building's grimy exterior, the stained bricks, and the peeling white paint on the trim looked more derelict than ever.

"It's just a shame," Helen told Tommy on the Friday before Thanksgiving as he was unlocking the door to the newspaper. "The Barton Building looked better unoccupied than it does now."

"Give her time," he said as he opened the door for Helen. "Rome wasn't—"

"Yes, yes." She pushed past him toward her desk. "Spare me your clichés."

Tommy knew Helen was still stewing over his recent conversations with Garth Price. She wouldn't come out and say so, but Tommy knew she thought he was making a huge mistake to consider selling the place. "What's the harm in just kicking the idea around?" he'd asked her on Monday morning, right after he'd admitted to spending a good part of Saturday with Garth. Helen's response had been to simply roll her eyes, then busy herself with making coffee. The next few days had felt like a standoff. Now that it was Friday, he was hoping for some sort of truce.

"Are you going to stay mad at me forever?" he asked as she tucked her handbag beneath her desk.

She stood, straightened her jacket, and gave him her receptionist smile. "Of course not."

"Come on, Helen," he urged her. "You're the closest thing to family I have. I can't stand having you acting like this."

"Really?" She peered intently at him. "You still consider me family?"

"You know I do. You're like a second mom to me."

"You planned to throw your *second mom* out on the streets?"

He frowned. "Out on the streets?"

"By selling the paper." She folded her arms across her front.

"Oh, Helen." He held up his hands.

"Don't 'oh, Helen' me, Tommy Thompson. I've given you some of the best years of my life, and this is the thanks I get? You go selling the newspaper behind my back?"

"I'm just talking to the man. I haven't made any deals yet. Besides, he'd be a fool not to keep you on, Helen. The paper wouldn't be the same without you."

"And without you?"

He ran his fingers through his hair and moaned. "I don't have time for this right now. We have a paper to get out."

"It's Friday," she reminded him.

"Still, there's work to be done." He knew she could see right through him, but at the moment it was all he had. As much as he loved and appreciated Helen, he knew she didn't understand him as well as she assumed she did. Her answer had always been to say, "Just roll up your sleeves, Tommy. Lose yourself in your work. Put out a good paper. You'll feel better in the morning."

Helen had always adhered to the myth that time could heal a broken heart. For the most part, she was good at keeping up the appearance that time had healed hers. But sometimes, when she didn't know he was looking, he could see the sadness in her eyes. Rich Fremont had hurt his wife deeply when he'd left her for a neighbor woman. Tommy suspected Helen would never be fully over it. But he had to give it to her, she was pretty good at hiding it. Much better than he was.

To sell or not to sell . . . that was his question. Garth Price's initial offer hadn't even been worth considering. Tommy had expected him to lowball him, especially after the way Tommy had complained about the paper initially. But after Tommy took the time during the weekend to really show Garth some of the town's charm, as well as the less obvious but positive aspects of the old newspaper, Garth's interest as well as his budget had increased. By Sunday he'd made a firm and fair offer, and Tommy told him he'd need at least a week or two to fully consider it. Now the first week was drawing to an end and Tommy still wasn't sure.

He looked out his window and frowned. The same trappings and trimmings of Christmas that brought joy to many usually made him more depressed than ever. He was tempted to close his blinds, but it was such a gray day that the little bit of light coming in right now was welcome. He looked at the Barton Building and shook his head. What was that woman thinking? If she wanted to cover her windows, she could've at least done it a bit more attractively. Matilda Honeycutt was a strange one, he'd decided.

Since Monday, he'd been trying to get together with her, but each time she had come up with an excuse. He could tell she was just trying to keep him at a distance, and at first he'd suspected it had to do with whatever sort of mystery business she planned to open up in there. But as the week had passed with even more resistance, he began to question if she really planned to open a business. Based on her evasiveness, he had his doubts.

Most legitimate businesspeople were eager to partner with the newspaper. They appreciated getting whatever free publicity they could, and he tried to accommodate them, hoping that they in kind would purchase more advertising from him. That's how it usually worked. But yesterday when he'd dropped by to see Matilda on his way to lunch, she'd almost treated him like an intruder. He'd actually planned on inviting her to lunch—his treat. If she'd been just a little friendlier, he would've done so. To be fair, it was possible that he was getting Matilda's responses mixed up with that loose cannon Rose, who'd been helping her. For some unexplainable reason, Rose had taken a deep dislike to Tommy the first day he'd walked across her clean floors. He could almost understand that. No one liked having their work messed with.

His second run-in with Rose made him suspect that her hostility toward him might be related to her daughter-in-law. Maybe he'd looked at the pretty city manager with a bit too much interest or appreciation. But was that any reason to treat him like vermin? Anyway, he did plan to get to the bottom of this whole thing—the question of who Matilda was and what she was up to, as well as why Rose had placed Tommy on her most-hated list. He figured that today's interview with the new city manager would be key.

He'd meant to do some research on Susanna yesterday, but thanks to Garth's interest in the newspaper, Tommy ended up spending most of his "slow" day rounding up all the bookkeeping facts and figures for the business for the last five years. He'd spent the whole afternoon making copies of things like utility bills and tax records. He would've asked Helen's assistance but knew exactly where that would get him—even deeper in the doghouse.

He had mixed feelings about today's interview. On one hand, he was eager to see Susanna again. He had put on his best khakis and a navy cashmere polo sweater that Helen had gotten him for Christmas last year. In fact, he was surprised Helen hadn't mentioned it this morning. Well, except for the fact that he was number one on her bad list just now. Maybe she and the other women should start a club. Which brought him back to the other hand—he didn't really want to see Susanna again.

Tommy had no doubt that during this morning's interview with Susanna, his question regarding her marital status—was she or was she not married—would be settled once and for all. Based on his experience with Susanna's mother-in-law, he felt fairly certain she was. To his surprise, that disappointed him—a lot.

Although he would never admit this to anyone, and as irrational as it sounded even to him, Tommy had decided that if indeed Susanna Elton was married, he would immediately sell the newspaper to Garth Price, but only for top dollar. He would apologize profusely to Helen, and then he would use the proceeds from the sale to travel the globe and perhaps get a job as a foreign correspondent—he was willing to work for pennies. Then for the rest of his life he could live as a vagabond in countries that never celebrated Christmas!

He was still ruminating on these discouraging thoughts as he went to get his usual morning coffee. As he was stirring in a teaspoon of sugar, Helen accosted him. "Tommy," she said urgently, "I was just looking into your new buddy Garth Price."

"What?" He dropped the stir stick in the garbage and looked at her.

"Do you know what he does?"

"You mean besides journalism?"

She shook her head. "He works for a big news corporation that purchases small-town newspapers and turns them into online papers."

"Huh?"

"Kind of like *USA Today*. Only it's online. The local news stories slowly disappear, and the hometown papers all end up homogenized and boring."

"Really?" He frowned. "He never told me any of that."

"I already emailed you some of the websites," she said.

"Thanks, I'll be sure to check them out."

"Now?" She looked at him expectantly like she wanted him to jump right on it.

"Not right now." He took a sip of coffee.

"Why not?"

He glanced at the clock above the stove. "Because I'm on my way to do an interview."

"An interview?" She looked skeptical. "Don't tell me Matilda Honeycutt finally gave in to you?"

He shook his head.

"Who then?"

"The new city manager."

Her eyes lit up. "Susanna Elton?"

"That would be the one." He took another sip, avoiding her eyes.

"I met her daughter last week. Nice girl."

"Yes, I've met her."

"I also met that mother-in-law." Helen's eyes got wide. "She is a real piece of work."

"Yeah . . . I met her as well."

Helen studied him closely. "You certainly look handsome today, Tommy. I noticed you're finally wearing that sweater I got you last Christmas. About time. Looks very smart too." She narrowed her eyes. "Why are you suddenly so concerned about appearances? Does it have anything to do with the city manager?"

"What do you mean?" he asked innocently. "Isn't she married?"

Helen's mouth twisted to one side. "I don't really know. I thought I'd heard she was divorced. But why would she have a mother-in-law in tow if that were true?"

"Good question. I'm sure before the interview is done, I will find out the answers for inquiring minds like yours."

"Didn't you do *any* research on her at all?" Helen sounded suspicious. "You know, there is this tool we use nowadays, Tommy. Some folks call it the World Wide Web. Really handy too."

"I was busy . . . with other things."

She nodded. "Oh yes, that's right. You've been busily trying to dismantle a newspaper that your father and grandfather worked hard to build from the ground up, a newspaper that the good citizens of Parrish Springs have grown to depend on and appreciate. You've been busily making dirty deals behind closed—"

"Yeah, yeah," he said quickly. "Please, spare me the drama. I'm already running late."

"Well, you better check out those websites I sent you,

Tommy." Her voice held the same warning he remembered from childhood whenever he came close to treading in her beloved flower beds. "Because I'd sure like to know who I'm working for before I head out to Julie's house for Thanksgiving next week."

"That's right!" He smacked his forehead. "I nearly forgot. What days are you taking off again?"

"If you'd read your email, you'd know." She shook her finger at him.

"I do read it. Just not yet today. When are you leaving anyway?"

"I'm taking *all next week* off," she said with exasperation. "Not that I'll be missed much by someone who plans to sell the place right out from under me. Good grief, will you even be here by the time I get back?"

"Oh, Helen!" He rolled his eyes and shook his head. "I've got to go."

"Well, it's been nice knowing you, Tommy. Don't forget to write. And don't forget to read your email!" she yelled after him as he left the kitchen.

"I told you I'm on it, Helen." He hurried back to his office to gather his jacket and notebook. Not his computer notebook either. Tommy still liked doing interviews the old-fashioned way, taking notes via shorthand in a little black notebook. He pulled on his brown leather jacket, tucking the notebook and his favorite pen in the roomy chest pocket. *Traveling light* is what he liked to call it. Free from the bulk of a briefcase or computer. But the truth was he was traveling with a very heavy heart.

Despite Rose's best efforts to be clandestine when it came to anything related to Matilda Honeycutt, Susanna had discovered the nature of the business Matilda planned to open. In spite of the predictions of the local gossips, it was not going to be (1) a tattoo parlor, (2) one of those import stores that reeks of incense and diesel, (3) a New Age shop selling drug-related paraphernalia, or (4) a disrespectable massage parlor.

Although Susanna was partly relieved the gossipers were wrong on the worst suspicions, she still felt worried. Partly for Matilda, because she actually liked the woman, but even more so for the town, because she knew that none of the merchants on Main Street would be particularly happy to see a second-hand shop. It was bad enough that thrift stores weren't zoned for this neighborhood, but with the Christmas shopping season upon them and everyone's hopes elevated in the expectation of some bright, shiny, consumer-friendly store, a secondhand shop was more than just a minor letdown. Furthermore, Susanna knew that the powers that be, including Councilman Snider, would now have the opportunity to make Matilda miserable.

"Why don't they just let her be?" Rose had said that morning after Megan left for school. "Who cares if she runs a thrift shop or not? This is a free country, no?"

"It's a free country, Rose, but you know there are ordinances. Businesses must apply for licenses, and a secondhand shop requires a special permit. According to my assistant, Matilda hasn't applied for one yet."

"Matilda knows what she's doing," Rose said.

"I hope so."

Rose gave a sly grin. "Besides, you can help her."

"I can?" Susanna filled her commuter coffee cup.

"Sure you can." Rose nodded. "You run the city, don't you?"

Susanna laughed. "More like the city runs me."

"Well, Matilda is a good person. I know you'll take good care of her."

"I'll do my best."

For that reason, Susanna had spent an hour trying to soften up Hal in the permit department, explaining that Matilda had been distracted getting her shop in order and overlooked applying for the permit.

"Well, she better get to it," he warned her. "We usually require two weeks to process a permit."

She smiled at him. "I know that and you know that, but I also know you can put a rush on it if needed."

"I can't make promises, Ms. Elton."

"Please, call me Susanna. Everyone else does."

He smiled. "Okay, Susanna. I still can't make promises, and I sure can't do anything if she doesn't come in here and apply."

"I'll do everything I can to get her in here today," Susanna assured him. "I really do appreciate your help with this, Hal. My hope is that Parrish Springs will become known as a can-do city and will attract some new business and commerce our way."

He nodded. "I hope so. I still feel bad for the layoffs a couple years back. I'd like to see some of those people come back."

"So would I." She thanked him again, then headed back to her office. Hopefully Hal meant what he said, but for all she knew he could just be another member of Councilman Snider's Good Ol' Boys Club. She couldn't believe how many people the old councilman carried around in his back pocket. It must be crowded in there!

On her way to her office, she stopped by the restroom and ran a brush through her hair and even put on some fresh lip color. She didn't know if Tommy was bringing a photographer with him or not, but she'd worn her favorite red suit just in case.

She knew it was possible that she was primping for another reason. For the past week, she had thought about Tommy quite a bit, more than she cared to admit. She even managed to discreetly discover that he was in fact single. Never married at all, her elderly neighbor had told her. Naturally, that surprised Susanna. She'd learned that if a man had never married by this stage of the game, there was usually a reason. But from what she could learn without looking overly interested, Tommy was fairly well respected by everyone. Still, she wasn't dumb—there could be other reasons.

She'd been thrilled when he'd called Monday afternoon to schedule an interview with her, but then dismayed when she checked her calendar. The only time that worked for both of them was Friday morning. For the past four days, she'd hoped to bump into him somewhere in town, but despite her best efforts to be out and about, their paths had never crossed once. Maybe it was fate. Or perhaps God was trying to tell her something. She'd be smart to listen. For now she was simply looking forward to seeing him again.

She was back in her office and just starting to get impatient when Alice buzzed her. "Tommy Thompson's here for the interview."

"Send him in," Susanna told her. She looked at her watch. He was only four minutes late, but for some reason it had seemed like longer.

"Sorry to be late," he said as he caught her still looking at her watch. "You know that commute from the newspaper office to city hall is killer this time of morning."

She chuckled as she stood to shake his hand. "I was thinking about that same thing as I drove to work this morning. I live less than three minutes from here—really, I should be walking—but the funny thing is I still bring my commuter cup in the car with me." She pointed to the shiny aluminum cup on her desk.

"Small-town life is hard to beat."

"I'm sold." She nodded to the chair across from her desk. "Make yourself comfortable, Tommy. We have just a little less than an hour."

He pulled a notebook from his inside coat pocket. It was a brown suede blazer that looked well made and expensive. He removed his jacket and casually laid it in the other chair, then sat down. Susanna noticed he was wearing an attractive navy sweater, probably cashmere. Well, the guy had taste.

He took the cap off of a silver pen, then smiled at her. "Ready?"

She blinked. "Is that all you use? Pen and pad? No electronics?"

He nodded. "I'm an old-fashioned kind of guy. This works for me."

"Interesting." She almost confessed that she was an old-fashioned kind of girl, but that felt like too much information. "Ready when you are. Fire away."

He started with the usual queries about educational background and past work experiences, but gradually the questions grew more personal. Not that she minded. She had nothing to hide. Not really. She explained that she'd grown up in a somewhat unconventional family. "My maiden name was Garcia, and my father was fourth-generation Mexican American with a Stanford degree in engineering. He worked for the city too. My mother was a blue-eyed, blonde beauty with no college education. She'd grown up in a dysfunctional family and really didn't want to be married. Consequently, my parents divorced when I was four and my father raised me."

"That is a bit unconventional, but interesting." He continued writing, glancing up occasionally. She wondered how he was really getting all this down because, as usual, she was talking fast.

"My father saw to it that I got a good education, and I suppose I kind of followed in his footsteps by working for city government."

"Your father sounds like a great guy."

She nodded. "He was. He died shortly after Megan was born."

"I'm sorry."

"Thanks. At least he got to see his granddaughter, and . . ." She paused to weigh her words. "He didn't have to witness me going through my divorce." She shook her head. "I know that would've hurt him deeply. Especially since he was the one who introduced me to my ex-husband."

Tommy nodded with a sympathetic expression. "How long ago was that? Your divorce, I mean. Well, not that it matters . . ." He seemed uncomfortable. "That doesn't need to be in the article. I didn't—"

"It's okay. I don't mind telling you, but I agree it probably doesn't need to be in the article. Megan was three when our marriage really began to deteriorate. In Carl's defense, his family had been a bit dysfunctional too."

"How so?" Tommy looked up from his notebook.

She smiled. "You've met my mother-in-law."

"Yes . . ." He seemed to be wearing a poker face.

Susanna couldn't help but chuckle. "Rose was the healthy part of Carl's parents' marriage."

He looked somewhat surprised, but to her relief he was not taking notes.

"As you may have noticed, Rose is Hispanic. However, Carl's father was not. He met her in Mexico, and she was quite a beauty in her day. They were one of those couples who married too hastily, if you know what I mean."

"I think I get your drift."

"Rose put up with a lot of grief from that man." She shook her head, unwilling to say too much. "And Carl . . . well, you know what they say. The apple didn't fall too far from the tree."

"I see."

"Carl and I parted ways, and Rose came to live with Megan and me." She stopped talking, feeling alarmed at how much she'd just revealed. "I would appreciate it very much if that remained in this room."

He looked directly into her eyes. "You have my word on it."

"Thank you." She sighed. "I don't usually run off at the mouth like that."

"Really, it's okay. You can trust me, Susanna."

"Yes, I think I can."

They moved on to city business. He asked her about the challenges of being a woman in a job that had previously been held by men, how she was adjusting to small-town life, and what had been her biggest challenge so far.

"I've only been here a couple of months," she began carefully. She wanted to say something quote-worthy without stepping on any toes. "I think the biggest challenge is striving to bring people and ideas together in a peaceful manner so that we can work together for the good of the entire city."

He chuckled. "Spoken like a true politician."

"Off the record?" she asked.

He closed his notebook. "Absolutely."

"This whole thing with Matilda Honeycutt is turning into quite the three-ring circus."

He nodded. "I've noticed. I have a feeling the fun hasn't even begun."

"Have you been able to interview her yet? Has she told you much about what's going on? What she's doing?"

"I've tried, but with the resistance I get from her and Rose,

I feel like I'm ramming my head against the big brick wall of the Barton Building."

"Well, I've got my concerns about her."

"Such as?"

"Off the record—although I'm sure it'll be public knowledge before long—I'm worried that she's going to open a thrift shop without the proper permits in place. At least that's what my mother-in-law is saying. Of course, Rose can't see anything wrong with it, but she doesn't know about Councilman Snider." She bit her lip, wondering what would happen if Rose and the councilman went head-to-head. It would be ugly.

"Councilman Snider will have a heyday with Matilda if she does that. He's just waiting to get his hands on that building."

"Believe me, I know." She nervously fingered the edge of the budget packet that she needed to take to her next meeting.

"Plus the other retailers won't be too pleased about a secondhand shop going in there. Most of them had been hoping for a furniture store. We haven't had one in town for years."

"I wish that were in Matilda's plans . . . but I'm afraid it's not."

"Well, I hope you can help her to sort things out."

"So do I." Susanna looked at her watch. It was time to wrap this up. "I really do like her, and I want to see her business succeed. But not at the expense of the other downtown merchants. That wouldn't be fair."

"Quite the balancing act." He stood, reaching for his coat.

"You got that right." She stood too. "Thanks for respecting my time, Tommy."

"No problem."

She wanted to say something more, like when would it be

her turn to ask him some questions, but it was time to get to the budget meeting.

"If you don't mind, I'd like to email you the article before it runs so you can make sure I've gotten my facts straight."

She pointed to his black notebook. "I have to admit that I'm a little curious about how that's even possible. I've been told that I can talk a mile a minute, and I doubt most people can write that fast."

"I use shorthand."

She laughed. "Well, of course you do."

They said goodbye, exited her office, and continued in opposite directions. She was a little concerned about how candid she'd been with him—she was usually more cautious with her words. But he'd promised she could trust him. She would have to see if Tommy Thompson was what he appeared to be—a man who kept his word. She sure hoped so.

Helen never worked a whole day on Fridays. But she had wanted to stick around long enough to hear Tommy's response to the websites she'd sent him. Surely he wouldn't continue his conversation with Garth Price once he realized what that shyster was really up to, would he?

She paced in the small kitchen, glancing up at the clock from time to time. It was 12:30 and Tommy still wasn't back. She'd already cleaned the coffeepot, sink, and counters, and unless she cleared out the refrigerator, which probably needed doing, she would have no excuse to stay.

She looked out the window just as Matilda Honeycutt was about to go into her building. That gave Helen an idea. Tommy had been trying and trying to make an appointment with that woman, but she'd been dodging him like he was with the IRS. Perhaps Matilda would be more open to talking woman to woman about her plans for her new business. If Helen was able to extract some information from Matilda, she might be able to pin down Tommy and make him listen to her.

With this mission in mind, Helen grabbed her purse and hurried across the street. Without hesitating, she knocked loudly on the door.

"Come in," Matilda said as she opened the door.

"Are you open for business?" Helen tried to mask her surprise at this unexpected friendliness.

"It all depends." Matilda smiled as she stepped aside. "But you are more than welcome to browse through the merchandise if you'd like."

"Thank you," Helen said. "I'd love to look around."

"Just let me get the rest of the lights turned on," Matilda said, "so you can see better."

Helen followed her, watching as Matilda's long, colorful skirt swirled behind her as she walked. Something jingled—probably jewelry—and her long, curly gray hair hung in a loose ponytail, tied midway with a loopy piece of purple cloth. Her feet shuffled along the wood floor, not bare today—but wearing sandals in mid-November? Truly, this was a strange sort of woman. But for some reason, Helen felt intrigued by her.

"There we go," Matilda said as the lights flickered on. "Let there be light."

Helen looked around the room. Much of the original shelving—the same sturdy wooden units that had been used for Barton's Stationery Store long ago—was still in place. Sure enough, there seemed to be merchandise arranged on the shelves. But there didn't seem to be any particular order to the way the goods were laid out. A baseball mitt sat next to a crystal vase with a black pocketbook on the other side of it, and next to that was a worn rag doll. Really, it made no sense.

81

What made even less sense to Helen was that this was obviously a thrift shop—exactly what Parrish Springs didn't want or need in this part of town. There were plenty of secondhand stores on First Avenue. Helen could only imagine how the other downtown retailers would react to this news. In fact, it seemed clear that there really was a story here. After years in the newspaper business, Helen knew that controversy always equaled story. She could already imagine the headline: "Local Merchants in Uproar."

"When do you plan to officially open?" Helen asked as she pretended to browse along the oddly stocked shelves. She picked up a chipped and stained coffee mug with the words "Coffee Brake" on it—was that a typo or was it supposed to mean something? Seriously, who would want this junk? She'd been to garage sales with a much better selection than this. She set the mug down.

"I think perhaps I'm already open," Matilda said lightly.

Helen turned in time to see Matilda pulling a piece of newspaper away from the window, then another. Slowly the afternoon light began to flood the room. But that seemed only to illuminate how shabby all the items on these shelves truly were. Helen didn't know what to say. She didn't want to be rude, but she couldn't help but think Matilda Honeycutt might be a few cards short of a deck.

Matilda stood on her tiptoes and stretched her short frame, trying to grab a piece of craft paper up high. She must have used a ladder to tape it up there because she was obviously unable to reach it now.

"May I help you?" Helen asked, wondering why she even bothered. Why would Matilda want for anyone to see inside here? Yet the next thing she knew, she was helping to reach the high pieces of paper, pulling them down from the windows so that the whole world could see the madness inside.

"Many hands make light work," Matilda said cheerfully as the last piece fell to the floor. "I'll take care of this little mess while you continue your shopping."

Shopping? Helen couldn't imagine what she could possibly want to purchase in this strange shop. Still, to be polite, and hoping she might learn something else about this eccentric woman, she continued her pretense of browsing. As she walked up and down the aisles, she could hear Matilda humming to herself as she disposed of the paper. At least she enjoyed her work. But did she think anyone would ever come in here to shop? For real?

After a bit, some nice music began to play. It sounded like Johnny Mathis and transported Helen back in time.

She paused. Despite the pleasant music, she was ready to exit this bizarre bazaar. She tried to think of a graceful way to make her getaway. She really didn't want to offend Matilda, who seemed a decent person, even if she was a little nutty.

As she stood there, Helen tried to read the lettering high on the wall but couldn't quite make it out. She used her glasses only for driving and didn't really want to dig them out of her handbag. Instead she squinted to read the curly letters and decipher the words, and finally she figured them out.

> *When disbursed seventy by seven, this*
> *precious gift is a slice of heaven.*

She wasn't quite sure what that meant, but something about the rhyme felt reassuring to her. In an odd way, it seemed familiar too. She just couldn't put her finger on it.

"How are you doing?" Matilda asked her. "Are you finding what you need?"

Helen turned and smiled. "I think that might be my problem. I don't really *need* anything."

Matilda's brow creased. "You don't need anything?"

Helen felt embarrassed. "Well, I suppose I do need some things. Like I need to go home and do the laundry." She laughed.

Matilda nodded. "We all have needs, don't we?"

"We certainly do." Helen was tempted to tell Matilda that she might need a good shrink, but that would be unkind.

"How about if I help you look?" Matilda offered. "Perhaps together we could find something you really do need."

Helen wanted to back up and say, "No thank you very much," but Matilda was already moving toward another aisle, saying she thought there was something over there, something that might interest her.

Helen felt a strange sense of fascination—seriously, what did Matilda suppose she had here that could interest Helen? Out of curiosity, she went over to where Matilda stood in front of a shelf not unlike the others, filled with a motley bunch of unrelated items. A dog-eared Webster's dictionary with no front cover, a pair of peeling patent leather shoes, a red plaid Thermos, and a set of warped plastic measuring cups that looked like they'd seen a few too many dips in the dishwasher.

"I, uh, I don't think there's anything here that . . ." Helen's voice trailed off as she continued to stare at the lopsided stack of measuring cups. They were Tupperware, lime-green, from around 1978 unless she was mistaken. Helen had owned an identical set at one time, back when she still used Tupperware products. She must have purchased hundreds of dollars' worth of the stuff back in the late seventies and early eighties.

Helen picked up the smallest measuring cup and stared as if hypnotized as the lime-green blurred and faded. Instead of old Tupperware, she saw Joanne Spencer. She saw her exactly how Joanne had looked when she first moved in next door—a painfully thin divorcée with dishwater-blonde hair and pale blue eyes that looked frightened. Helen had befriended her neighbor, and when Joanne began to sell Tupperware to make ends meet, Helen had hosted a party to help her out. As it turned out, Joanne had helped herself to Helen's husband when he went over to help with a clogged sink drain. Their affair lasted for nearly ten years before Helen figured things out. Naturally, she threw Rich out—and Joanne took him in. Eventually they left town, and Helen threatened to kill them both if she ever saw them again.

"What do you think?" Matilda asked, jerking Helen back to the present.

"Think?" Helen looked at Matilda with wide eyes.

"How do those work for you?"

Helen looked back at the measuring cup still in her hand. It was trembling. Or perhaps her hand was trembling.

"Old things sometimes contain old stories . . . unfinished stories . . . don't you think?"

Helen didn't know what to think. She looked back at the measuring cups and felt that old feeling of hatred sweeping through her again. Not just a trickle either, like it usually was. Today it came at her like a tidal wave. Had that much anger been inside her this whole time?

She leaned her head back, seeing once again those curly-lettered words high up on the wall. She read them out loud this time. "'When disbursed seventy by seven, this precious gift is a slice of heaven.'" She looked at Matilda. "What does that mean?" She pointed to the sentence. "That saying up there?"

"What do you think it means?"

Helen frowned. "It sounds somewhat familiar. That 'seventy by seven' part, I mean." She thought hard. "I used to go to church for many years . . . I think maybe it's in the Bible."

Matilda nodded but said nothing.

Helen looked back down at the little green cup and suddenly saw Joanne again—and she felt that deep-rooted hatred. In a flash she knew exactly what those words meant. "Seventy times seven" was how many times Jesus Christ had told his disciples to forgive others. She turned and stared at Matilda. "Is *that* what it means?"

"What?" Matilda asked.

"Forgiveness. That's what it means, doesn't it?"

Matilda just smiled as she picked up the other measuring cups. After nesting the smallest one on top, she gave the stack to Helen. Cupping her hands around Helen's, she said, "You take these, dear, and you think about it. I'm sure you'll figure it all out." Humming to herself, Matilda walked away.

Helen stood there for a long moment, trying to make sense of everything. Feeling slightly dizzy, she finally walked out of the store and just stood there. With the cups still in her hands and her thoughts spinning back to more than thirty years ago, she walked back to the newspaper office and got her things. It wasn't until she was inside her car and nearly home that she realized she'd never even paid for the measuring cups. Did that make her a shoplifter?

Once she was home, safe inside the same house where she'd once used an identical set of measuring cups in her kitchen, she set the cups on the counter and just stared at them. She still remembered the morning she'd gathered up her Tupperware products and thrown them all over Joanne's front yard. That same morning, she'd thrown all of Rich's clothes and personal items onto their own front yard. Later that day, she had the locks on the house changed.

Compared to all the things she'd wanted to do—horrible things she'd fantasized about doing—her actions were quite subdued. For the next few weeks, she'd spent hours planning elaborate murders, fires, accidental deaths . . . It had consumed her, devoured her, threatened to destroy her. Until Tommy's mother had stepped in and put a stop to the madness.

Somehow Betty had managed to get Helen out of her funk. Betty had spoken of forgiveness, and out of respect for their friendship, Helen had listened. But it was a pretense. When Betty got sick a few years later, Helen became even better at pretending. For Betty's sake, she acted like she harbored no ill feelings toward Rich and Joanne. The truth was she had hated them both. She still hated them now. She had never forgiven either of them.

Betty was right—holding back forgiveness came with a high price. Even if Helen could hide her bitterness from others, cover it up, pretend it was gone, it festered away inside of her, and in her darkest moments, it would raise its ugly head and torment her some more. Helen was sick of it.

She picked up the smallest measuring cup and went to her room, closed the door, got down on her knees, and just cried—long and hard. Then she did something she hadn't done in years. She prayed. With that little green cup in her hands, she asked God to help her forgive the two people who had wounded her the most deeply. "Help me to forgive Rich and Joanne," she sobbed. "Help me to move on and be free of this poisonous burden." She prayed like that for about an hour and eventually fell asleep.

When she woke up, she felt different. Happier, freer, lighter, as if a heavy weight had been lifted from her heart. She thanked God for helping her and set that little green cup on her bedside table as a reminder. She put the biggest green cup in her kitchen window and the half cup in a drawer in the den, and the quarter cup she planned to take to work and set on her desk.

Each time she saw one of those lime-green cups, it would be her reminder that she'd forgiven Rich and Joanne, that she was free of them and that bitter monster of unforgiveness. Even if she had to forgive them again and again—even seventy times seven—she was determined to do it. With God's help, she would do it.

On Friday afternoon, the Johnson Sign Company showed up at the Barton Building and hung a big sign. In bright green and red and all caps, the words THE CHRISTMAS SHOPPE now hung above the front door. By Saturday midday, the rumor spread like wildfire that Matilda Honeycutt was out of her head—certifiably nuts.

"Nothing but a bunch of worthless old junk in there," people were telling each other. "And that crazy lady calls it a Christmas store!"

"Something's got to be done," George Snider told several of the business owners as they met for coffee on Sunday morning. This impromptu meeting had been initiated by the councilman. "You can't let one business ruin the downtown atmosphere, and especially right before Christmas."

"That's right," one merchant said. "I peeked inside there yesterday afternoon, and the trash in that shoddy little shop makes Marty's Secondhand Stuff look like a boutique."

Everyone laughed.

"It seems irreverent to call that place a Christmas shop,"

Lauren from the shoe store said. "I call it a little shop of horrors."

"It's bad enough she's a newcomer, but to do something like this is almost like spitting in our faces," Ben Marshall declared. "My family's owned our hardware store for five generations, and I'm not about to take this sitting down."

"What do we do to get rid of her?" Cindy from the Clothes Horse asked. "I'll do anything to help."

"Should we circulate a petition?" someone else asked.

George waited contentedly as the group kicked around a number of ideas. Some good. Some not so good. He wanted to be sure they really got their ire up, and then he made a suggestion. "A petition isn't a bad idea—or perhaps just a letter signed by all the downtown merchants to show you're all united in this. Make plenty of copies of the letter, and be sure to come to the city council meeting tomorrow night. Be there early so you can sign up to address the council." He chuckled. "The more the merrier. I'll make sure the press is there as well. And make sure you choose a spokesman to present the letter with the signatures." He nodded to Ben. "You'd be a good candidate for that."

The others agreed, and Ben seemed glad to help.

"What should the letter say?" Cindy pulled a small notebook and pen out.

"State the facts," George told her as she made notes. "Say that the local merchants are offended that the city would allow a thrift store in a part of town where it's clearly in violation of zoning and permit ordinances. Demand that this wrong be righted immediately. Make sure you take one copy of the letter to the city manager's office, stating that you want to hear a response from her at the meeting as well."

"Is that enough to get rid of that woman?" Ben asked.

"It should shut her business down," the councilman told him. "I expect it'll just be a matter of time before she moves on."

They talked for a while longer. George felt confident that their effort would do the trick. He predicted that Matilda Honeycutt would be out of business before Thanksgiving. Still, he would pay her a visit on Tuesday afternoon. Playing the caring councilman, he would sympathize with her woes. Perhaps he'd even extend an olive branch and offer to help her find a more suitable location for her secondhand shop—over on First Avenue with the other lackluster shops. After all, he still had a listing in that neighborhood. It wasn't as large and needed some work, but Ms. Honeycutt might not mind.

After commiserating with her, George would be a gentleman by offering to take the Barton Building off her hands. If he was feeling particularly generous, he might even offer to pay the same price she'd forked over. Although he was tempted to lowball her. But, he reminded himself, the holidays were coming. Plus she'd cleaned the building up a bit, and that was worth a little something. And knowing that he himself had a generous buyer for the building . . . well, he could afford a little generosity too.

As the councilman sat in the coffee shop rubbing his hands together, Rose was puzzling over the lack of business in Matilda's new shop. She'd stopped by to say hello and browse a bit. She wasn't sure there was much here to really interest her, but she liked Matilda and she liked a bargain. She also liked the music Matilda had playing in here—very upbeat. Unless Rose was mistaken, it sounded like Mexico's Pioneer Mariachis. She hadn't heard that group for ages and wondered if it was possible to buy their CDs somewhere.

"Are you having a good day?" Matilda asked Rose as she came over to join her.

"I guess so. I was just wondering why there are no customers in here, Matilda. There are plenty of shoppers in town today." Rose picked up a crystal vase, but seeing a chip, she set it back down. "I could hardly find a place to park. I just don't know why they're not at least stopping here to check out the new business."

"They'll come," Matilda said.

Rose realized something as she turned a little cow-shaped creamer upside down. There seemed to be no prices listed on anything. "Where are the price tags?" she asked.

"Did you find something to interest you?"

Rose studied the creamer, then set it down. "Not really. I just don't see any prices."

Matilda pointed to the wall, at one of the odd sayings Megan had helped her to paint last week.

> *The sweet value of this treasure*
> *is impossible to measure.*

"What does that mean?" Rose mentally translated the words into her mother tongue, but that didn't seem to help much either.

"What do you think it means?"

Value you cannot measure? It made no sense to Rose. Everything had a price, didn't it? "Does that mean I'm supposed to make an offer if I find something I want?"

"Something like that. What is it that you *want*, Rose? What is it worth?"

Rose frowned and shook her head. "I, uh, I don't know."

"I mean, what do you *really* want?" Matilda peered at her.

Rose wanted to say there was absolutely nothing here that she wanted, but seeing Matilda's lack of business and knowing that Matilda might very well be her only friend in this snooty little town, she bit her tongue. For Rose, that was not easy.

"Walk with me," Matilda said. "Perhaps we'll find something together."

Rose felt almost as if she were under Matilda's spell as she followed her through the quiet shop. Then Matilda stopped, and Rose didn't know what to do. Matilda seemed to be staring at something. Then, almost as if her eyes had just been opened, Rose saw it too. A familiar piece of Mexican pottery—a small, colorful canister just like her abuela had when Rose was a small girl. Except that this canister had a crack in it and was missing its lid. Other than that, it was identical. The same blue and yellow flowers. Rose picked it up, feeling the weight of the piece in her hands. It felt lighter than she remembered . . . but she had been just a little girl then.

"Rose," Abuela had scolded her. *"Donde está el caramelo?"*

Rose had hidden the candy behind her back at first, then realized that Abuela knew exactly what she'd been up to, sneaking candy from the canister while the old woman's back was turned. Rose held out her hand, revealing her sweet, stolen treasure. Abuela simply shook her head, returned the candy to the jar, and gently lectured Rose on the virtues of patience and why Rose needed to learn to wait. Abuela reminded Rose that she had planned to give her a caramel after Rose finished her chore. Not before. She told Rose that those who were willing to wait usually got the best things in life, but those who refused to wait usually wound up with nothing. Nothing but heartache. *"La paciencia,"* she had said. *"La paz."*

"La paciencia," Rose now said aloud. *"La paz."*

"Patience," Matilda said quietly. "And peace."

"Yes." Rose nodded. "That's right." Her grandmother had been telling her that patience was like peace.

Matilda pointed up to the words on the wall again.

> *The sweet value of this treasure*
> *is impossible to measure.*

"What do you think peace is worth, Rose?" Matilda asked.

Rose stared up at the words. "Impossible to measure?" she murmured.

Matilda patted the cracked canister still in Rose's hands. "You keep this, Rose. A gift."

"Gracias." Rose nodded with tears in her eyes. Without saying another word, she left, but as she went down the street, she wondered what had just happened. Was it magic? Was it a mind trick? Was Matilda a witch like some townspeople said? It made no sense at all! How had Matilda known about Abuela's canister? Rose had never mentioned that little tale to her or to anyone. Of course, Rose's lack of patience was no

secret, but how did Matilda know how she felt inside? How did she guess that Rose had no peace in her life?

Rose carefully set the canister on the passenger seat, putting her handbag next to it to protect it from rolling. She even took the time to buckle up her seat belt, something she did only when Megan was along because Megan always nagged her. She took her time to look for her keys, and she didn't even swear in Spanish when she couldn't find them at first.

As she started her car, she felt strangely calm. As if there was really no need to hurry, which was so unlike her since she was always in a rush. But she knew that the last thing she needed was another speeding ticket, so for a change she drove slowly through town. When a car sat too long at the traffic light and Rose was about to blast the idiot with her horn, she stopped her hand in midair. Really, what good would that do?

Rose parked her car, then cradling the canister in her arms, she carried it to the tiny house that sat a ways back from the larger house where Susanna and Megan lived. It had once been a carriage house but was now Rose's little nest. She went inside and set the canister on the mantel above the little brick fireplace. She hadn't even used the fireplace once—partly because it hadn't been too cold yet, but also because she knew that to start a fire and keep it going took time and patience, which she never seemed to have enough of. But tonight she would make a small fire, just to see if it worked. Perhaps she'd even make herself some hot chocolate. Something she might do for Megan or Susanna, but never just for herself. She decided she would use a good china cup to drink it from too.

Easing herself down into the comfy floral chair that Susanna had gotten for her a few years ago, Rose put her tired feet on the ottoman and leaned back into the cushions. She would be seventy in December. Seventy years old—that was older than her sweet abuela had been when she passed on! If, at Rose's age, she couldn't slow things down some, practice a little patience, experience a bit of peace . . . when in the world could she?

She closed her eyes and thought of dear Abuela again. Rose wasn't naive. She knew there had been many difficulties in her grandmother's life. But when times got hard, Abuela never threw a fit—not like Rose usually did. Instead Abuela would get out her rosary, close her eyes, and silently pray. When she finished her prayers, the expression on her brown, wrinkled face would be as peaceful as an old nun's.

After her nap, Rose planned to search through her still-packed moving crates. She would locate Abuela's old rosary and give it a try.

11

Susanna couldn't put her finger on it, but something about her mother-in-law was different. She was quieter than usual and strangely calm. Susanna was reminded of the feeling in the air shortly before a thunderstorm hit. Knowing Rose, that was probably a possibility.

After Megan left for school on Monday morning, Susanna was tempted to ask Rose about her mood change. Except she knew Rose hated being questioned about anything personal—that alone could set her off. Besides, Susanna reasoned as she refilled her coffee mug, if Rose had something to tell her, she would do it in her own sweet time. In the meantime, Susanna would embrace the "ignorance is bliss" motto and enjoy this small pocket of peace.

As it turned out, her peace was short-lived. She'd barely stepped into her office when Alice tapped on her door with a grim expression. "Ben Marshall has left a couple of phone messages."

"Ben Marshall?" Susanna tried to remember why that name was familiar.

"He owns the hardware store," Alice said. "Seems that he and some of the other downtown merchants have organized themselves."

"Organized themselves?"

"To see that Matilda Honeycutt's new business is shut down."

Susanna let out a groan. "That was sure fast."

Alice nodded. "They have a valid point. Matilda's not zoned or licensed for a secondhand store. I did what you said on Friday and tried to make the laws clear to her in regard to her permit. I even offered to help her to petition for an exception. But she was, well, sort of vague."

"She's actually opened her store up?"

"Haven't you seen it?" Alice asked.

Susanna shook her head. "I took Megan to the city on Saturday. I'd promised her we'd have a mother-daughter day of shopping and a play."

"Sounds lovely."

"It was. Then I spent most of Sunday holed up at home, going over the new budget proposal."

"Not so lovely."

"But back to Matilda. She's opened for business already then?"

"Yes. She even put up a sign. A big one. It's actually rather nice, and I felt hopeful at first. It's called the Christmas Shoppe. I thought perhaps . . . well, that it might have Christmassy things, like decorations or gifts or . . . you know?"

"I know," Susanna admitted. "I was hoping the same thing."

"I peeked in the window Saturday afternoon, and it's just

all that old junk you saw in the boxes. Only now it's spread out on the shelves as if it's real merchandise, like things people would actually want to purchase. Only it's just these weird and unrelated items." Alice smiled sadly. "It's really kind of pathetic."

"Oh dear."

"I like Matilda," Alice continued. "I just don't get it."

"Join the club."

"It's like she's setting herself up to fail. Even though she got a good deal on the building, she could've found a cheaper property over on First Avenue. She could've opened up a legitimate business there."

"I know." Susanna shook her head as she flipped through the mail. "I don't get it either."

Alice stepped fully into the office now, closing the door as if wanting privacy. "I don't like to say this, Susanna, but it almost makes me wonder if she's not trying to sabotage the city."

"Sabotage the city?" Susanna stood up straight, looking curiously at her assistant.

"I know, it sounds paranoid. But I've heard stories of people who come to a city with a plan."

"What kind of plan?"

"Like they'll try to break a relatively small ordinance, like zoning or a business license. Then they'll turn it around to make it seem like the city is persecuting them. All the while they've got some high-powered attorney waiting in the wings. Or worse yet, the ACLU. All they're trying to do is get a settlement and—"

"Oh, I don't think Matilda is really like that," Susanna

said quickly. But what she didn't admit was that she'd had this exact same fear already.

"No, of course not." Alice still looked uneasy. "Whatever the case, I told Ben Marshall that you could see him at 9:40. That gives you about fifteen minutes before your meeting with the mayor."

"Thanks." Susanna looked at her watch. "I think."

"At least Ben will have to keep it short," Alice pointed out.

"Right." Susanna thanked her again, then used the few minutes she had before Ben's appointment to check her email. To her delight, there was a message from Tommy. It seemed he'd already written his piece on her and had attached it for her approval. She was just finishing up the first-rate article when Alice announced that Ben Marshall was there to see her. As it turned out, Ben had brought friends.

"Come in," Susanna told the small group with serious faces. She smiled as if this were a social visit. "What can I do for you?"

Ben cleared his throat, then presented her with what appeared to be a letter and a petition. "This is from the downtown merchants," he began. In a formal tone, he proceeded to inform her of their indignation that the city would allow a secondhand store to open in the middle of town. "To make matters worse, it's being run by an outsider. Someone who doesn't understand Parrish Springs or our fine history. I think the city should bear some of the blame. Not only for allowing her to open a business like that, but for selling her such a valued property in the first place."

Susanna listened, waiting for Ben to finally wrap things up.

"I appreciate how you and the local merchants have put this into writing," she told him. "I will be giving this situation my full attention." She smiled at all of them, wishing there was an easy way to change the gloomy atmosphere they'd brought into her office. "Just so you know, the city has *not* permitted a secondhand store in the Barton Building. I'm unsure as to whether there's been confusion on the part of Ms. Honeycutt, but I am sure we'll resolve this."

"When?" asked Cindy, the owner of the Clothes Horse.

"As soon as possible." Susanna gave them her business smile.

"It's our biggest season of the year," Cindy continued. "Matilda's shop is so out of place. It just cheapens the whole downtown area. It's a disgrace."

Susanna forced another smile. "But the Clothes Horse is such a lovely shop. I can't imagine how it could be cheapened by anything."

"You know what they say," Cindy countered. "It's all about location, location, location. If my shop looks like it's located next to a frowsy thrift shop, then it makes it look like my merchandise is second-rate too."

"I do understand your concerns," Susanna assured them. She pointed to the clock on the credenza. "I have an appointment with the mayor at ten. In fact, I might even mention this to him—"

"Don't worry," Ben said quickly. "We already hand-delivered a copy of this letter to the mayor, as well as to all the city councillors. We're on it."

"And we'll be at the city council meeting tonight," another said.

"I see." Susanna nodded. "It sounds as if you've put together quite an attack plan."

"That's right," said an older man she didn't know. "Councilman Snider has been very helpful. I didn't even vote for him last term, but maybe I'll be voting for him next time." He chuckled.

As Susanna gathered her things, she thanked the group for their time.

"We'll see you tonight then," Cindy told her.

"It's a date," Susanna said lightly.

But as she walked to the mayor's office, she felt anything but light. In fact, she was borderline angry. Councilman Snider certainly wasted no time in rallying the local merchants. She could only imagine what kind of backroom meeting he'd thrown together. It didn't take a mentalist to guess what the old boy was up to. He wanted that building badly, and he would probably go to great lengths to attain it.

As she waited for the mayor's assistant to finish her phone conversation, she knew better than to mention this particular element of the Honeycutt dilemma to the mayor. Not only was he a member of the Good Ol' Boys Club, he and Councilman Snider were golf buddies, or as her old boss used to say, "thicker than thieves."

"Good morning, Susanna," Mayor Gordon said as she sat down in the chair opposite his desk. "How's life treating you these days?"

She made the usual friendly small talk, keeping it brief and not overly personal. Spotting a copy of the letter from Ben and his downtown buddies in the center of the mayor's desk, she decided to jump right in. "I see you got your copy of the letter too," she began. "Their committee was just in my office."

Mayor Gordon frowned. "They stopped by here too. Is it true what they're saying?"

She pressed her lips together. "It's partly true. And it's partly a matter of perspective." She quickly explained what had transpired.

"So you can handle this on your end?" he asked.

"I plan to." She nodded confidently. "However, you should be warned."

"Warned?" He frowned.

"Ben and friends will be attending the city council meeting tonight."

Mayor Gordon groaned. "Just what we need."

"I know." She sighed.

"I was hoping to actually wrap some things up tonight."

"Well, I'll do what I can today to resolve this. Maybe we can put the whole thing to rest before it gets too out of hand."

"Hopefully." He changed the subject to go over their usual weekly agenda, but she could tell he was trying to cut it short. Finally he said, "I'm not going to take too much of your time, Susanna. My hope is that you can put a lid on this thing before it really starts to boil. You know the holidays are upon us. Thanksgiving is just days away. The timing on this ridiculous secondhand store couldn't be worse." He shook his head. "What is wrong with that woman anyway?"

Susanna had no answer to that but said, "Perhaps . . . do you think it would help if you paid her a visit?"

"Me?" He looked surprised.

"As a goodwill gesture. Maybe you could reason with her. She might respect that the mayor of our city took the time to befriend her and help her find a solution to this."

He looked thoughtful, then finally nodded. "You know, Susanna, that is not a bad idea. If it works, it wouldn't be bad PR for the mayor's office either."

"Not at all."

He nodded. "Okay, then I'll give it a whirl."

"Good for you."

He glanced at his watch. "In fact, I don't have another appointment until after lunch. So if we're done here . . ."

"As far as I'm concerned." She stood.

He chuckled as he saw her out of his office. "I've seen that Matilda Honeycutt around town a few times. Strange bird. My wife says she's just an old hippie. That may be so, but I had some friends like that back in my college days, before I met my wife. It's not something I usually talk about, but I was a bit of a rebel back then. A nonconformist, if you know what I mean."

She smiled. "I never would've guessed that, sir."

"Oh yeah. I had some wild ideas back in my day. I have to hand it to her, I mean, that someone my age—anyway, that's my best guess—would be comfortable enough in her own skin to go around town looking like *that*." He shook his head with a bewildered expression. "Of course, that was one thing back in the sixties. Can you imagine what folks would say if I went around with long hair and sandals and love beads now? They'd be thinking the mayor had lost his mind." He laughed.

Susanna laughed too. As she returned to her office, she tried to imagine Mayor Gordon dressed like he'd described, but it was impossible. She'd never once seen the mayor in anything less formal than casual business wear. Still, it would be highly amusing.

"What are you smiling about?" Alice asked as Susanna stopped by her desk.

"Oh, nothing." Susanna gave Alice a list of tasks to complete before this evening's council meeting. "Mayor Gordon is going to talk to Ms. Honeycutt now, but I still want to do everything I can—get our ducks in a row—just in case this turns into a battle zone tonight."

"I'm on it," Alice promised.

Susanna returned to her office to go over the budget some more. By lunchtime, she was feeling extremely curious as to how the mayor's visit had gone. Not only that, but she was determined to try once more to talk some sense into Ms. Honeycutt before this got any further out of hand. She hurried over to the Barton Building, arriving just in time to see the mayor emerging.

Susanna blinked, seeing that he had an old catcher's mitt with him. In fact, he was actually wearing it, along with a very odd expression—sort of a dazed-looking smile.

"Mayor?" she said.

He looked at her as if trying to place her face. "Oh, Susanna," he finally said. Then he chuckled. "That reminds me of a song." He broke into singing, "'Oh, Susanna, don't you cry for me. 'Cause I come from Alabama with my banjo on my knee.'" He laughed as if that were hilarious.

"How did it go?" she asked him, trying not to question his sanity.

"Just great," he said.

"She's willing to close the business?"

"Well . . . uh . . . I don't know." He looked perplexed. "I'm not really sure."

"But I thought you—"

"I have to get going," he said as if he were suddenly uncomfortable about something. "I've got some unfinished business to take care of. If you'll excuse me."

"Of course." She watched as he hurried away, the catcher's mitt still on his hand like he was late for a ball game.

Weird. Very weird. Susanna supposed that it was up to her to negotiate this thing with Matilda. Her plan was to come at her positively but firmly. Unless Matilda was a fool, she should see the sensibility of Susanna's suggestions.

Preparing a little speech inside her head, Susanna opened the door and cautiously entered. She could handle this. It was her job to handle it. Diplomatically but with authority, she would inform Matilda that there was a better place to locate a business like this, and she would assure her that they would find a perfect building for her business.

However, Susanna had barely opened her mouth before she began to feel that she was participating in a scene from *Alice in Wonderland*.

"A *perfect* building for my business," Matilda echoed her.

"Yes," Susanna said. "We could find a—"

"Perfect is unrecognizable, Susanna. You find it only when you quit looking. The harder you try to hold on to it, the easier it slips away."

"I mean a place that's zoned for secondhand."

"The second hand moves quickly, dear. The longer you wait, the harder it is to catch it."

"I mean your *thrift* shop, Ms. Honeycutt."

"Please, call me Matilda. And a thrift shop it is not. The real treasures of this world cannot be purchased with any sum of money. But they can be given away for free."

"Please," Susanna said firmly. "I'm only trying to help you, Matilda, but I need your cooperation. You need to understand that there are people who want to drive you out of business . . . out of town, even."

"No one can drive me where I do not wish to go, Susanna. Not in a car or in a truck or on a camel. Don't be worried about me, dear. Really, I wish you would continue your shopping. I haven't even had my lunch yet, and I'm—"

"I didn't come here to shop," Susanna said.

"Of course you did. You just forgot what you were looking for. Perhaps you just need some—"

"I'm not here to shop," Susanna repeated. She frowned. "Can't you understand that I'm not looking for anything here today?"

Matilda's pale eyes opened wide. "Are you saying you have everything you need in this life? *Everything?*"

Susanna considered this. "Well, no, of course not, but I just—"

"Then go ahead, dear. Feel free to browse . . . just as long as you like. I'm sure you'll find something you can use, if you'll just be open to looking."

"But I—"

"I'll even give you some privacy." Matilda walked toward the back room, her bracelets jingling as she left the otherwise quiet room.

Susanna wanted to scream. Instead she turned around and exited the building. Seriously, that woman was crazy!

In all his days of living in Parrish Springs, Tommy had never seen anything like what he was witnessing at tonight's city council meeting. He was a wordsmith, and even he couldn't find the vocabulary to describe it. Mental-illness terms like *schizophrenic* and *bipolar* came to mind. Yet he couldn't use words like that in his news story. He scratched his head and listened as Mayor Gordon spoke in Matilda Honeycutt's defense again.

"I understand your concerns," the mayor was telling the head of the lynching committee (Tommy's nickname for Ben Marshall tonight). "But I feel you haven't really given Matilda Honeycutt a fair shake."

"A fair shake?" Ben retorted. "What about—"

"Please refrain from your rebuttal until your turn," the moderator reminded Ben.

"This woman has been in our town only a short while," the mayor continued. "I think it's hasty on the part of the community to attempt to give her walking papers so soon."

"What about the laws?" someone from the back of the room shouted.

"Order!"

"All I'm suggesting," the mayor said in a surprisingly patient tone, "is that we let Matilda Honeycutt continue her business until the end of the year. I plan to help her petition for a—"

"She's put you under her spell," a woman's voice called out. "That Matilda Honeycutt really is a witch."

Several others started to chime in. Not everyone was calling her a witch, but most of the comments were unfavorable. However, there were a couple of people who, like the mayor, were trying to defend Matilda.

"Order!" the moderator shouted for the umpteenth time. "You people will come to order or security will escort you out!"

The mayor attempted to continue his speech about tolerance and timing, but again and again he was interrupted until finally the meeting was abruptly ended, and with the help of security, the mayor hastily exited the room. After he was gone, a few of the councillors, including Councilman Snider, remained behind. They volunteered to "continue the conversation" by fielding comments and questions "off the record," but it was clear that the speakers simply wanted to rant and vent.

"I'm not calling her a witch," Cindy from the Clothes Horse said, "but she is definitely a troublemaker." She waved to the crowd. "Look at us. This is that woman's doing. We've never fought like this before."

"You just don't understand her," another woman said.

"You don't know what she's doing, and you won't even give her a chance to show—"

"This is about the law," Ben said. "We can't allow her to come in here and break it like she's doing."

"That's right," Councilman Snider agreed. "If we don't respect the law, we will have nothing but anarchy. Cindy is right. Look at us tonight."

"The holidays are upon us," Lauren from the Shoe Inn added. "Not only is our shopping season at risk, but so are our peace and goodwill toward men."

"What kind of goodwill is it to throw a newcomer out of town just because she wants to run a different kind of business?" someone else said.

On and on it went until Tommy felt his head was spinning. For the first time in his reporting history, he wished he'd brought a handheld digital recorder with him. There was no way he was getting all these quotes. His article, at best, was going to be as much mumbo jumbo as this crazy meeting.

Thankfully, someone at city hall finally had the good sense to turn the houselights out. He glanced around the council chambers, now eerily lit by the green glow of the emergency exit signs, trying to see if he could spot Susanna Elton. Her seat up front was vacant, and he suspected she was the one responsible for cutting this brouhaha short.

"Anyone who wants to keep discussing this is invited to my place," Councilman Snider offered.

"You mean anyone who wants to help with your witch hunt," someone said.

As they were exiting the chambers and the building, the argument continued, with a pause outside at the foot of the city hall stairs. Tommy considered joining the group at the councilman's house, but he had a headache that was growing worse. Besides, he could guess what people would say. More and more of the same.

As he headed for the parking lot with the group not far behind him, another mental-health label hit him—*obsessive-compulsive*. That is what they were. It was like they were stuck in a rut and couldn't let it go. All they could think was that Matilda Honeycutt was the enemy and it was up to them to rid their fair city of her evil presence.

Tommy knew there were two sides, sometimes more, to every story, and rather than wasting his time at the councilman's house, he intended to get the other side of this one. He planned to start with Matilda Honeycutt herself. He wished she had come to the meeting tonight, wished that she'd been present to speak out in her defense or at least explain what she was up to. However, as he was about to get into his car, he thought she was probably wise to have avoided it. Who needed this kind of chaos?

"Hello?" a female voice called quietly from the shadows.

He turned to peer across several cars, spotting Susanna Elton in the shadows of a streetlight. She was waving and looking as if she were trying to be discreet. Maybe, like him, she was fed up with the drama.

"Who are you hiding from?" he whispered as he joined her.

"Councilman Snider," she whispered back. "He wants me to join them at his house, says it's my responsibility to come."

"Your responsibility to whom?"

"The city. He says it's my fault this is happening."

"Why?"

"He blames me for Matilda Honeycutt—all of it."

"Oh." Tommy rolled his eyes. "I think I get it."

"His car is parked next to mine, and he's right back there. I'm waiting for him to leave before I go."

"I see." Tommy peered into her eyes. They looked even darker and bigger in this dim light, and they seemed a little frightened. For some unknowable reason, this made him want to protect her. "Want to hide out with me?" he offered.

"Hide out?"

"My car's right there. We could get coffee or something. Then I could bring you back after the rabble-rousers are gone."

"Coffee sounds lovely. Do you mind?"

"Not at all. It might help my headache." He led her to the car, hurried to open the passenger door, and waited for her to get in. Feeling like James Bond, he rushed around to the other side and hopped in, starting the engine.

"You have a headache?" she asked with sympathy.

"I'm not sure if I had it before the meeting or if it's the result of the meeting."

"I can understand how tonight's insanity would give anyone a headache."

"Insanity," he repeated. "That's exactly how I wanted to describe it." He told her how he'd been fixated on mental-health disorders tonight. She laughed, and for some reason that made his head feel a little better.

Soon they were seated in a quiet booth of the coffee shop, and together they tried to make heads or tails of tonight's crazy meeting.

"What boggles my mind more than anything is the mayor," Tommy finally said. "I've never seen him act quite like that."

"I know." She nodded her head. "It was weird. Almost like he was in a dream, or maybe just dazed." She told Tommy about finding the mayor with a catcher's mitt outside of the Christmas Shoppe and how he sang "Oh, Susanna" to her. "It was truly bizarre," she confessed. "Straight out of *The Twilight Zone*."

Tommy tried to wrap his head around that. "You probably don't want me putting that in the paper."

She blinked. "No, of course not. I can trust you, can't I?"

He smiled. "Yeah, sure. To be honest, I wouldn't even know what to do with that one. It is bizarre."

She told him about her own visit with Matilda today. "I only wanted to reason with her," she explained, "and yet she kept putting up these roadblocks. It was like she was playing mind games with me. I finally just gave up."

"What do you really think about her?" he asked. "Off record?"

Her brow creased, and she sat quietly for a long moment. "I don't know for sure. Initially I liked her and I wanted to help her. I still want to help. Especially after hearing some of those horrible comments tonight. But I just don't understand her. It's like she doesn't care . . . like she doesn't even want my help."

"Maybe she's just independently wealthy and eccentric."

"Maybe." Susanna frowned. "Or maybe it's something else." She told him about her assistant's theory. "I don't think she's right," she said quickly. "Matilda just doesn't strike

114

me as malicious or evil." She shrugged. "But then, I've been accused of being naive more than once."

"You don't seem naive to me," he told her.

"Really?" She looked into his eyes. "What do I seem to you?"

He considered this. "You seem very smart. And careful. Although . . . I have to admit that tonight you seemed a little bit scared."

She looked worried. "Did it show?"

"Not so anyone else would notice. I guess I was looking harder."

She seemed slightly relieved. "The truth is I am worried."

"Why?"

"Why?" Her brows arched. "This is my job, Tommy. I'm the city manager, and now it looks as if I've managed the city right into a nasty dispute—and right before Christmas too. According to Councilman Snider, I've messed up. Badly."

"Oh . . . I see."

"And I have a child to support. I moved us here, including my mother-in-law, who has been acting strangely lately. I have good reason to be worried. Don't you think?"

"I don't know."

"You don't think Councilman Snider could make my life miserable?"

He chuckled. "He can make anyone miserable. But here's what got my attention tonight—for the first time in a long time, Councilman Snider and Mayor Gordon are on opposite sides."

She nodded slowly. "Good point."

"A point that might count for you."

She smiled. "Thanks. I needed that morsel of encouragement."

"Thank *you*. I think I must've needed this late-night coffee break, because my headache is nearly gone now."

"Glad I could be of service."

He held up his empty coffee cup. "Care for another round?"

She peeked at her watch. "I should probably get home. Rose is with Megan, but it's late, and . . ."

"I totally understand." He stood and, to his own surprise, actually reached out his hand to help her up. Not that she needed help. It just seemed a good excuse to touch her, to connect. He hoped she wouldn't mind.

"Thank you." She smiled prettily.

Feeling as awkward as if this were a real date, he couldn't think of one more thing to say. They silently walked to his car, where once again he opened the door, waiting for her to get in.

"You're a dying breed," she told him as he was about to close her door.

"What?"

"Gentlemen these days are hard to come by."

"Oh." He smiled. "Thanks."

They were both quiet as he drove back to city hall. The parking lot was vacant now. "Here we go," he told her as he pulled right next to her car. A sensible white Subaru wagon.

She thanked him again as he opened her door and helped her out. "Would it be forward of me to ask what you're doing for Thanksgiving? I'm sure you must already have plans by now."

The truth was he planned to eat Thanksgiving dinner at

the same place he'd eaten for years—his best friend Darren's home—but instead of admitting this, he simply shrugged.

"You don't have plans?" she asked.

"Not really."

"Then please join us!"

He smiled. "Sure. I'd love to."

"Oh, that's great. It'll be Megan and Rose and me, as well as a couple of other singles I invited from work. I'd love to have you there."

He was a little disappointed about the "other singles" bit but decided it was better than nothing. "Can I bring anything?"

"Are you kidding?" She laughed. "Remember Rose? She has it all under control. No, just come, and bring along plenty of patience since you know how she can be."

He nodded. "Will do!"

"Oh yeah, I almost forgot. Great article. You made me sound much smarter and nicer than I really am."

"You might need it too," he said, then wished he hadn't.

She sighed. "You could be right about that. Anyway, I do appreciate it."

"That reminds me, I'm sending a photographer to get some shots of you at work tomorrow. Is that okay? I asked him to set it up with your assistant."

"Sure. Thanks for the heads-up." She waved as she got into her car.

Tommy watched as she drove away. For the first time in a long time, he felt a real sense of hope, like maybe there was more to life than what he'd been experiencing this past decade or so . . . like maybe there really was a light at the end of this long, dark tunnel. Or perhaps he was simply doing it again—getting his hopes up just high enough to have them smashed down to smithereens again. Only at this stage of life, at his age, he doubted he could take it. Especially during the holidays!

Tommy hadn't really meant to eavesdrop on Tuesday afternoon. He simply wanted to get a quote—even just one short, succinct sentence—from Matilda Honeycutt. He wanted it before it was time to put the paper to bed. He'd gone into her shop, which appeared to be open, but not seeing her about, he'd ventured to the back room. Eventually he wandered upstairs and tapped lightly on the door to her apartment. He had to get a quote. Not just for his article or for the townsfolk, but for Matilda too. So far she had distanced herself from the fray. It seemed only fair that she should be able to have some words from her own lips printed in her defense.

Dismayed at not finding her, he'd gone back down the stairs, then stopped. He could hear what sounded like Councilman Snider loudly lambasting Matilda. Tommy remained in the shadows to listen. If nothing else, he could use this eyewitness incident to help open the eyes and hearts of the people of Parrish Springs.

"Some might think me coldhearted to come in here two

days before Thanksgiving," he told her. "But you need to hear what I have to say, Ms. Honeycutt. The sooner you understand it, the better it will be for all. I felt sorry for you to start with. I even offered to buy you out of this mess. But would you listen? No. So now I'm here to tell you that we are onto you. We know you're practicing some kind of voodoo witchcraft in here. And whatever you've done to the mayor is going to bring you down. Do you hear me?"

"My hearing is fine."

"Fine! So you need to understand that today I am offering you exactly what I offered the city when I tried to buy this building before. This is a onetime offer, do you understand that?"

"I do understand," she said sweetly. "But do you understand?"

"Understand what?" he demanded.

"That you have come into my shop yet I do not see you doing any shopping."

"Shopping?" he boomed. "Why in tarnation would I shop here?"

"Because I think I have what you are looking for."

"Don't be trying your wily ways on me, Matilda Honeycutt."

"We are all looking for something . . . searching . . . Some of us have been searching since childhood." Her voice had a soothing quality to it, almost hypnotic. Perhaps it was working on George as well, since he was no longer yelling. Tommy heard the shuffling of feet, almost as if someone was dancing, and he peeked out to see that they were simply walking. The councilman was following Matilda with a bewildered expression, and she continued to talk in that soothing way, saying how searching was a good thing and how people should never give up, no matter how old. "You can always find what you're looking for," she continued, "if you're willing to keep looking."

"I don't know . . . What do you mean?" the councilman asked in a much calmer tone.

Tommy was still peeking from the shadows, suddenly feeling like a voyeur and a trespasser. He was afraid to come out and reveal himself now, worried about how bad it would look. Feeling like a kid caught in the middle of a freeze-tag game, he just stood there. Matilda and George were behind some open shelves now. All Tommy could see were parts of their backs, but he could still hear their voices.

"See up there?" Matilda was saying.

"Up where?" he asked gruffly.

"The writing . . . on the wall."

"'Sometimes so bright it's hard to see, this dear gift will set you free.'" He cleared his throat loudly. "What does that mean?"

"What do you think it means?"

"I don't know," he snapped.

"Just relax and let it come to you. You're an intelligent man."

"Something bright . . ." he began slowly. "It's hard to see . . . and it sets you free?"

A light went on in Tommy's head. *The truth.* Those words described the truth. He was suddenly reminded of his parents. His mother would say things like, "Shine the light of truth" in order to expose something. He'd also heard his father say, "The truth sets you free." But what did the riddle really mean? Who was it for? George Snider?

"Where did you find this?" the councilman asked in a choked-up voice. "How did you know about it?"

"You found it yourself," she told him. "You were willing to look, and now you found what you needed. This is the gift that will set you free."

"I don't know," he stammered. "What do I do with it?"

"You *know* what to do with it," she said gently.

"What if I don't want it?" he asked. "I don't want it. You take it back."

"No, no, it's yours, George. You take it with you."

"But I—"

"Please don't turn down a gift, George. You might not ever get another chance. Today is here now. It's yours for the taking. Please, just take it."

The next thing Tommy heard was the sounds of steps, the front door opening and closing, and then silence. He was wishing Matilda had gone out with George, but he was pretty sure she hadn't. He felt like a little boy who was about to get caught—how was he going to explain hiding out like this? Eavesdropping on what sounded like a very personal conversation.

He weighed his options. He could simply confess his bad manners and beg her to give him a quote. But getting her cooperation now, especially under these embarrassing circumstances, seemed highly unlikely. Or . . .

He glanced at the back door. He could make a run for it. While he didn't like to think of himself as a coward, running did seem a good option. He could blame his childish behavior on undercover reporting. After all, paparazzi were notorious for grabbing a story then hitting the road. Not that he liked comparing himself to the bottom-feeders of journalism. And it wasn't like he planned to write about what he'd just witnessed—he most certainly did not.

As he burst out the back door into the alley, he couldn't help but wonder, *What just happened?*

As Susanna set out her best china on the dining room table, she was trying not to let thoughts of Matilda Honeycutt spoil her Thanksgiving Day. Really, why should she concern herself with that stubborn, thickheaded woman? So what if she lost her business? If Matilda didn't care, why should Susanna?

It was Rose's comment that had set Susanna off. It seemed Rose had actually invited Matilda to join them for dinner today. "She flat-out refused to come," Rose had told Susanna this morning as she was getting the turkey ready to go into the oven. "She even admitted she didn't even have any other plans." Rose shook her head. "I don't understand that."

"Maybe she's not a social person," Susanna said a bit sharply.

"Oh no," Rose protested. "Matilda is social. Very social. You just don't know her like I do."

Susanna hadn't questioned this. For one thing, she didn't want to start an argument on Thanksgiving, although that seemed unlikely since her mother-in-law had been amazingly calm and controlled this week. Susanna couldn't figure that one out. In fact, she was starting to get a little worried. She'd heard somewhere that a quick transformation in personality or temperament could be symptomatic of a brain tumor. Surely Rose didn't have cancer?

Susanna didn't have time to think about that today. Despite Rose's claims that she didn't need any help with fixing dinner for eight, Susanna insisted that she and Megan were going to help. As a result, it was like a three-ring circus in their kitchen as the three generations attempted to make pies, prepare stuffing, stir the gravy, and mash the potatoes.

"Enough!" Rose finally shouted as Susanna spilled half the gravy on the counter. Rose threw both hands in the air and looked like she was about to explode into Spanish cursing, which might've been a relief, considering all the other worries tumbling through Susanna's mind. Instead Rose simply closed her eyes and took a deep breath while Megan and Susanna exchanged concerned glances.

"I'm sorry, Mija," Rose told Susanna. "I will finish up in here. You must now go and see to your guests."

Susanna was tempted to protest, reminding her that Alice was doing a great job of playing host to Jeremy and they were the only two here so far, but she knew better. "Okay." She nodded as she removed her apron. "I can take a hint."

"*Gracias!*" Rose rolled her eyes as she grabbed a sponge.

Susanna was reluctant to disturb Alice and Jeremy in the family room where they were watching football and visiting. Susanna had been playing matchmaker with these two for weeks now and had in fact "accidentally" invited both of them early for this purpose. "Well, I was just officially kicked out of my own kitchen," she told them as she joined them in front of the TV. "Who's winning?"

Just as Jeremy was giving her the score and game update, the doorbell rang. Relieved to leave the two alone again, Susanna excused herself to answer it.

"Tommy." She opened the door wide. "Come in!"

He had a bouquet of flowers in one hand and a bottle of red wine in the other. "Am I early?" he asked.

"Not really," she assured him. "We're kind of laid-back about that."

"I thought about walking," he said as she set his gifts down and waited for him to remove his jacket. "I only live about eight blocks from here, but it looked like it was going to rain."

"I heard we might even see some snowflakes by the weekend." She slipped his brown suede jacket on a hanger. Resisting the urge to take a deep sniff—it had the sweet smell of leather plus something else equally as nice—she hung the jacket in the hall closet, then turned and smiled.

"We had snow right after Thanksgiving a couple years ago," Tommy said. "Made for an interesting Christmas parade."

"Seems like it would be pretty."

"You'd think so. But it was a little rough on the marching band when it turned into slippery slush. And you had to feel for those scantily clad majorettes."

She laughed. "Yes, they'd probably need their long johns."

She led him into the family room and introduced him to Alice and Jeremy. Sensing Tommy's eyes on her and feeling

126

inexplicably uncomfortable, she decided to excuse herself to the kitchen.

"Can I help in there?" Tommy offered. "You wouldn't know it to look at me, but I'm actually a pretty good cook. Comes with being a bachelor so long."

Susanna wasn't so sure. "Well, I guess we could see if Rose needs help."

"Rose . . ." Tommy looked a little uncomfortable. Almost as if he'd forgotten all about her cantankerous mother-in-law.

"She's actually not been herself lately," she explained as she led him toward the kitchen. "As in, she's been unexplainably congenial."

"Congenial?" He looked skeptical. "Interesting."

"Hey, Rose, do you remember Tommy Thompson?" Susanna said as she returned to the kitchen. She was curious as to how well Rose would control herself now. Her first encounter with Tommy had been nasty, and several times Rose had freely expressed her opinion on the newspaperman.

Rose started to scowl, then gave a crooked smile. "You're the rascal who tromped on my clean floors," she said.

"I still feel badly for that. Maybe I can make up for it by offering my help in here."

She looked doubtful. "I never met a man who was worth two cents in the kitchen."

"Tommy claims he's a good cook," Susanna said a bit skeptically.

Rose laughed. "That's something I'd have to see to believe!"

"Give him a chance, Abuela," Megan urged her.

Just then the doorbell rang again. Feeling guilty for abandoning Tommy, Susanna went off to welcome Margot and Rick. Both were in their thirties and from accounting. This time there was no matchmaking involved since she knew Rick was a confirmed bachelor and Margot had a fiancé serving overseas. Still, it had always been Susanna's habit to reach out to other singles during the holidays no matter where she worked, and here in Parrish Springs it was no different.

She lingered in the family room, visiting with the others and replenishing the appetizers. Finally, worried that Rose's unexpected calm might have worn thin by now, she ventured back into the kitchen just in time to see Tommy removing the turkey from the oven.

"At least he's strong," Rose told her. "Now we'll see if he can cut a turkey."

"Not until it's rested for ten minutes," he said as he removed his paisley oven mitts. "If you'd like, I could remove the dressing for you."

Rose looked surprised. "Maybe he does know his way around a kitchen."

Megan giggled.

"My mother, God bless her, taught me how to cook and clean and do laundry when I was just a kid."

"Really?" Megan looked impressed. "Abuela hardly lets me do anything."

"What are you saying, Mija?" Rose frowned. "You clean your own room. You help in the kitchen."

"But I don't know how to do laundry, and I've never cooked anything without your help."

Rose waved her hand. "Don't be in such a hurry, Mija. Patience, patience."

Susanna studied her mother-in-law closely. She had never heard her say anything like that before, and she wanted to question it. But she knew now was not the time.

Before long, they were all seated at the dining room table with Susanna on one end and Rose on the other. "Are you going to ask the blessing, Mom?" Megan asked.

"Yes." Susanna smiled. "Unless someone else wants to."

Since there were no other offers, Susanna bowed her head and asked the Thanksgiving blessing. As usual, she prayed specifically for each one at her table, asking God to richly bless them during the holidays.

"Thanks," Alice told Susanna. "That was very cool."

They all visited congenially as the food was passed around. Rose continued to be on her best behavior. While that was a relief on one level, it was also deeply disturbing. Susanna knew that once her guests were gone and Megan was occupied with the computer or TV, she might need to question Rose about this personality change.

Before long, and to Susanna's dismay, the conversation got stuck on Matilda Honeycutt and the Christmas Shoppe. "My sister was in there this week," Rick was saying, "and she said something very strange happened to her."

"Strange?" Susanna asked. "How so?"

"She wouldn't give me the specifics," he explained, "but she actually used the words 'life changing.' Can you imagine?"

"Life changing?" Alice frowned as she helped herself to

cranberry sauce. "Matilda's a nice enough person, but I don't get how she could change a life."

"Unfortunately, if Matilda doesn't make some changes in her own life, she's going to be out of business soon." Susanna instantly wished she hadn't said that.

"Susanna tried to talk sense into her about the zoning and permit issues," Alice told them. "Matilda refused to listen."

"Does she think she's above the law?" Margot asked as she ladled out some gravy.

"I heard the mayor has taken her side." Rick buttered his roll. "Maybe he'll work up some kind of exception for her."

"I don't see how, outside of changing the laws," Alice said, "and that can't be done without a referendum."

"Councilman Snider and the merchants group will fight it all the way," Susanna said. "Just like they did Monday night."

"We're going to have a nasty little battle on our hands." Alice reached for the salt. "Just what we need at Christmastime. So much for peace and goodwill."

"I don't like playing the heavy," Susanna said, "but I'm inclined to agree with the downtown merchants on this one. If Matilda refuses to cooperate with the city ordinances, I don't see any alternative. She's going to have to close her doors. The sooner the better."

As they continued kicking around this idea, Susanna couldn't help but notice there were two people staying out of the conversation. One, not surprisingly, was Rose. She did consider Matilda to be a friend. The other one was Tommy. A couple times he looked like he was about to say something and then stopped.

After everyone was sufficiently stuffed, they agreed to take a break before dessert. Susanna told everyone to make themselves comfortable, so some trickled off to the ball game and some to the library. When Rose finally shooed Susanna out of the kitchen, she decided to look for Tommy. She found him by himself in the library, looking at her bookshelves.

"See anything you like?" she asked as she joined him.

He smiled. "They say you can tell a lot about a person by their collection of books."

"What does this tell you?"

"You have a variety of interests." He pointed to a row of biographies. "You like reality and historical figures." He nodded to her section of cozy mysteries. "And you like a good escape."

She chuckled. "I wonder what I'd find on your bookshelf."

He seemed to ponder this. "Travel books. Science and technology. Thrillers."

She nodded. "I see."

They chatted lightly for a bit, and then their conversation grew more serious. "It sounds like you're taking a hard stance on Matilda these days," Tommy said quietly.

"I don't know what else to do," she told him. "She put up a roadblock when I tried to help her."

"I know . . . but maybe you should go about it differently."

"Differently?" She studied him. "You mean I should cater to Matilda? Don't forget that I happen to run the city, Tommy. I can't exactly go around giving in to the strange whims of some eccentric entrepreneur, can I?"

"I'm not saying give in, Susanna. I'm just saying maybe you

should give her a second chance before you decide to drive her out of town on her broomstick."

"I never said I would do that!"

"Not in those words," he said quickly. "That sounds more like Councilman Snider. But if you're aligning yourself with him, well, it's possible that his words could be confused for yours."

"What are you saying?" she demanded.

"Just that . . . well, you're new in town. Why not walk softly?"

"And carry a big stick?" she shot back.

He laughed, although his eyes looked serious. "No, that's not what I meant. I just meant don't be in such a rush to shut down something you don't fully understand."

"Are you telling me how to do my job?"

He held up both hands. "No, of course not. I was simply advising you. As a friend. I'm sorry if I—"

"I seriously doubt that you comprehend what a tightrope walk this has already been for me. No matter what I do, I am the bad guy." Frustration was bubbling up in her. "It almost makes me feel like this whole thing was a setup. Like Matilda moved here just to stir things up, create chaos, divide the city, and get me into trouble."

"You give Matilda credit for a lot."

"I'm just saying that's how I feel, Tommy. She's not helping matters either. She could cooperate with me a little. She could let me help her. Instead she wants to play games." Susanna clenched her fists. "Well, maybe it's time to play hardball with that woman."

He blinked. "Hardball?"

"Well, think about it. The Christmas parade is tomorrow. Shoppers will be out and about. Law-abiding merchants will be trying to make a living. Why should I allow one spoiler to sit in the middle of everything, spreading her toxic discontent and division? Like Alice said, she's stealing our Christmas cheer, and it's just not fair."

Tommy looked like he was at a loss. Not for the first time, Susanna regretted her years spent on the high school debate team so long ago. As hard as she'd worked on diplomacy, she still didn't know when to shut up sometimes. On the other hand, why was Tommy suddenly so defensive of Matilda Honeycutt?

"Do you know something about Matilda that I don't know?" she asked him. "Some reason I should cut her more slack?"

"No . . . not really."

"I read your article yesterday," she continued. "I didn't see any direct quotes from her. Weren't you going to give her the opportunity to defend herself?"

"The opportunity never actually arose."

"Maybe it didn't need to," Susanna continued, knowing she was probably sticking her foot in her mouth. "It seemed to me that your article took her side."

"Took her side?" Tommy looked surprised and a bit hurt.

"In my opinion, it did. Or perhaps you took the mayor's side."

"I do not take sides, Susanna." He frowned. "I keep my reporting impartial and save my opinions for the editorial page."

"So you say." She folded her arms across her front. It was

really weird, but for a moment she wondered if perhaps she and her mother-in-law had actually switched temperaments recently. Kind of like a version of the movie *Freaky Friday*. Only not so funny.

"I can see we don't agree on this." Tommy stuck out his chin. "I think it might be best to agree to disagree."

"Fine."

"If you don't mind, I think I'll excuse myself. I forgot about something I need to attend to . . . uh, at the newspaper. I hope you understand."

Now she felt horrible. What had she done? Was she actually driving him away? What was wrong with her? But instead of apologizing or backtracking, she simply nodded and said, "I understand perfectly."

She knew she should get his coat and see him to the door. She also knew that to do so would reveal just how vulnerable she felt. Why had she let her guard down? Why had she let him get to her?

To hide her feelings and her shaking hands, she told him goodbye, then turned and walked away. She went directly to her bedroom and closed the door. Taking in some deep breaths and trying to regain her composure, she had to admit that something about this was familiar. Painfully familiar. Despite years of therapy following the end of her miserable marriage, and despite her therapist's continual warnings that until Susanna dealt with some old wounds, she would continue to push away any man who got too close—even if that man turned out to be Mr. Right—Susanna knew that she'd done it again.

Tommy was a good guy, but he had gotten too close. He'd

been on his way to the secret chambers when her security alarms went off—all the bells and whistles. As a result, Susanna went into her usual defensive mode, and now the thick cement walls were up and the barbed wire in place . . . and God bless the man who was able to get over them.

Maybe it was due to the rain or the near-freezing temps, or, as a lot of merchants were saying, "Maybe it was due to Matilda (the witch)," but this year's Christmas parade was dismal, soggy, and cold. Not to mention attendance was way down. As a result, Black Friday's Christmas sales turned out to be unimpressive too.

By Tuesday, Tommy wondered if perhaps Susanna was right. Maybe Matilda Honeycutt and her faux Christmas store were hurting their town. He wanted to ask Helen what she thought of the latest developments, but after being gone last week, she seemed to be buried in catching up. The upside was that she no longer seemed mad at him. Even when he told her he was still unsure about selling the newspaper, she had simply shrugged and pointed out that it was his decision and she would support him no matter what he chose.

He'd been tempted to question her on that. Was she saying she would idly stand by if she thought he was making the mistake of his life? Didn't she care? But then, she'd been at her sister's home in Florida last week. Sometimes she talked of retiring there, so perhaps she was already making an escape plan of her own. Who knew?

All Tommy knew was that this town was getting gloomier by the day. As a newspaperman, he should welcome a good fight. But the truth was he never had before, and he didn't now. It was almost embarrassing to admit that. Especially when he was the one who always complained about small towns and the lack of interesting stories and events. How could he explain that even when there was a hot little controversy sitting right in front of him, he just wished everyone would forgive and forget and get on with it?

For that reason, he was getting irritated at Matilda. Not only was she tearing this town apart, she had managed to put a serious wedge between him and Susanna. Oh, he wasn't delusional. He knew that he and the city manager weren't in a real relationship. At best, they were just friends. Rather, they had *been* just friends. Now they were simply professional acquaintances. She'd made that clear at last night's "emergency" city council meeting when she'd given him a frosty smile and moved on.

He skimmed over the story he was working on—another installment of the Matilda-versus-the-downtown-merchants battle—and frowned. He was trying hard to be impartial. In all fairness, he felt that if he were leaning one way or the other today, it was definitely away from Matilda. Still, something was missing. He needed a quote from her.

"If anyone wants me, I'll be over at the Christmas Shoppe," he said to Helen as he pulled on his coat.

Her auburn brows arched. "Why?"

"Getting quotes if I'm lucky."

"Oh." She nodded. "Maybe more than that . . . if you're lucky."

"Huh?" He frowned at her.

She smiled. "Take your time, Tommy."

"Yeah, right. Never mind that we have a paper to get out."

She waved a hand at him. "Oh, we're doing fine. Don't worry so much. It'll make you old before your time."

He just shook his head, then went out. He felt the wind starting to whip up. They hadn't received any of the snow that had been predicted yet, but there was definitely a bitter nip in the air. He hurried across the street, and seeing the OPEN sign on the door, which seemed a joke since Matilda never seemed to care whether she was open for business or not, he let himself in.

As he walked inside, he saw old Mrs. Jarvis coming out. In her hands was a dog-eared children's book. But it was her eyes that got his attention. Misty and yet sparkling at the same time. Mysterious.

"Oh, there you are," Matilda said cheerfully. "I was wondering when you'd come back."

"Come back?" He cocked his head to one side.

She smiled. "Well, never mind. Here you are. Would you like to look around?"

"No." He shook his head as he pulled his little black notebook and pen from his chest pocket. "I'm not here to shop. I'm here for the newspaper. I'd like to ask you some questions."

She gave him a knowing look. "If you ask me some questions, does that mean I get to ask you some too?"

He shrugged. "I guess."

"All right." She strolled toward him. "How about if we walk and talk. That always helps me to think better."

"Uh . . . sure." He fell into step with her as she slowly strolled down an aisle. She paused to adjust a windup toy monkey, then continued.

"Do you see anything that suits you here?" she asked.

Without even looking, he shook his head. "No. As I mentioned, I'm not here to shop, Ms. Honeycutt. I came to—"

"Please, call me Matilda."

"Yes. Matilda." He clicked his pen. "I notice you haven't been to any of the city council meetings. Does that mean you're not interested?"

"Not interested?" She looked puzzled. "I'm very interested . . . in the people. But you're right, meetings don't interest me too much. I'm more of a one-on-one sort of person."

"So you're aware of what people are saying about you? The dissension your business is causing?"

She waved an arm. "Dissension? This little place? Oh, I don't think so."

"People are talking about you. Some say you're a . . . well, a witch or some kind of mystic. Do you have a response to that?"

She simply laughed.

"I'll take that as no?"

"What do you think I am?"

He peered at her. "I'm not sure, but I do think you're a little strange."

She nodded and continued walking. "What about you, Tommy? Who do you think *you* are?"

He paused, considering this. "Well, the obvious answer is that I'm a newspaperman."

"On the outside . . . but I'm talking about the inside, Tommy. Who are you really?"

He shrugged. "Just a regular guy, trying to figure things out."

"How are you doing with that?"

"What?"

"Figuring things out."

He was getting aggravated. "My turn for questions. Why do you refuse to cooperate with the city in regard to permits and such?"

"I did get a permit for my business before I opened my doors. Dear Alice in the city manager's office helped me."

"But it's the wrong kind of permit for a thrift shop."

She just smiled.

"Are you trying to be a troublemaker or are you just stubborn?"

Her smile faded. "Do you have any more questions?"

"What will you do when the city shuts this place down? Will you sell? Or move to another location?"

Her brows barely lifted as she made a tiny shrug. "When the time comes . . . you will see. But before that time comes, Tommy, are you sure you don't want to look around? Are you sure there's not something here that you can use?"

He glanced at the useless old junk cluttering the shelves. "I don't think so."

"Perhaps it's because you're not really looking."

"I have a paper to get out," he said as he closed his notebook. "I would've liked to have included more of you in this story, Matilda, but it's obvious you don't want to cooperate."

"Cooperation, as you say, is a two-way street, Tommy."

"Right . . ."

"I do hope you'll come back again," she called as he made his way to the door. "When you have more time to browse."

As he crossed the street, he decided that he absolutely agreed with Susanna. Matilda was certifiably nuts. She didn't seem to care if her business got shut down or not. He would try to keep his article unbiased, but it wouldn't be easy.

Back in his office, Tommy hammered away on his laptop. Done with the article, he was now writing an editorial, and he was letting his opinions fly freely. After all, what did it matter? If this was what life in Parrish Springs had to offer him, why not just sell the newspaper and be done with it? Helen didn't seem to care one way or the other now. And with Christmastime breathing down his neck, why should he stay and put himself through this holiday treadmill again?

He finished his op-ed piece and sent it to his design man, then picked up the phone. He was going to call Garth Price and tell him that he could have the paper, electronic or not. If Garth's offer was still good, the newspaper would be his for the taking. Tommy was done with Parrish Springs and the *Spout*. Maybe he'd head to someplace warm like Cancun or Hawaii.

Instead of calling Garth, Tommy called the city manager's office. He expected to leave a message, but the next thing he knew he had Susanna on the other end. "Oh," he said. "I'm sorry to bother you."

"That's okay," she said in a businesslike tone. "What can I do for you?"

"I just wanted you to know that I've come around to your side."

"My side?"

"Well, I've given up on Matilda. I tried my best to get something out of her for tomorrow's paper. She refused to cooperate. So . . . I guess you were right."

There was a long silence.

"I also wanted to tell you that I plan to sell the newspaper." He told her about Garth Price and his plan to go electronic. "I'll be moving on. Just in case I don't see you, I wanted to say goodbye, and to thank you for having me at your place for Thanksgiving. I'm sorry we got into that silly fight over Matilda Honeycutt." He let out a weak laugh. "See, I guess she really has divided this town."

"I'm sorry to hear that," Susanna said in a stiff-sounding voice.

"That Matilda divided the town? You said as much yourself."

"No, that you're selling the paper . . . and leaving."

"Well, I've been considering this for years, but the timing is right." He brightened his voice. "I'm ready to call it a day."

"Thanks . . . I mean for letting me know."

"No problem."

"If you'll excuse me, I'm late for a meeting."

He told her goodbye, but as he hung up the phone, he felt a heaviness unlike anything he'd felt since the December his mother had died and Victoria had dumped him. If anyone had asked him, he would've sworn it was impossible to feel that kind of sorrow again. Who knew history would keep repeating itself? Even more reason to blow this joint.

He put in his iPod earbuds and listened to the Bee Gees, imagining white, sandy beaches and tropical sunshine. He promised himself that it wouldn't be long until he left behind this place and all the sadness.

16

By Friday, Susanna was seriously fed up with Matilda Honeycutt, and she planned to tell her so in person. Not only that, she would present her with the letter of warning that Alice had put together for her. The city wasn't exactly bringing out the big guns yet, but it was getting close. Being a peacemaker at heart, Susanna hoped they could manage this whole thing without any more drama.

Bracing herself for Matilda's usual verbal merry-go-round, Susanna was barely inside the shop when she cut to the chase. "You are in violation of a city ordinance," she told Matilda as she held up the paperwork. "Unless you make some effort to comply, your shop is going to be shut down. Do you understand that?"

Matilda smiled sadly. "I understand what you're saying, Susanna. But is that really why you came here?"

"Of course it's why I came here. I want you to know how serious this is. Not only will you be shut down, you may also be fined and taken to court. The city attorney is already investigating this case."

"Yes, yes . . . but let's talk about you, Susanna. I have a feeling there is something here that you need. Won't you please just look around?"

"I did not come to look—"

"How about if we make a deal," Matilda said. "You look around and I will look into all you're saying."

Susanna blinked. "You will?"

Matilda removed the paperwork from Susanna's hands. "Let me get my reading glasses. I'll read this while you look around."

"Oh . . . okay." Susanna nodded. As Matilda went to the counter, Susanna pretended to browse the frowsy-looking shelves. Noticing what looked like bare spaces, she was curious as to how much merchandise Matilda might actually be moving. She was even more curious about who could possibly want this junk.

She paused to listen to the music now playing. For some reason she hadn't noticed it before, but it was an old Beatles song, one of her father's favorites, "Let It Be."

She hummed along to the tune as she looked at the odd items on the shelf in front of her. There was a pair of old ballet shoes, a woman's handbag with a broken strap, a dented metal pencil box with a picture of Mickey Mouse on the front, a set of dog tags that were so worn she couldn't even read the name . . . and then she stopped and just stared at the next object.

It was a simple, heart-shaped silver locket. The embossed flowers on the front were scratched almost beyond recognition, the clasp was broken, and there was no chain. But it looked exactly like the locket her father had given her for her sixteenth birthday more than twenty years ago. Yet she knew it couldn't possibly be the same one. Carl had destroyed that locket long ago. Just like he'd destroyed her heart.

Almost afraid to touch it, she reached her hand toward it, then pulled back. This was crazy. But her heart was pounding hard and she couldn't resist. She picked up the locket, and it was almost as if a jolt of electricity traveled down her fingers, through her arm, and into her chest. Breathing hard, she held on to the locket as the memory of Carl's fury swept over her. She had caught him in a lie—just one of many. Using his dark-eyed charm and handsome smile, he tried to talk his way out of it, but it was useless. When he realized she wasn't buying it, he hit her.

Even though her father had passed on more than a year before, Carl accused her of being a daddy's girl. He pointed to the locket she always wore and swore at her, saying that she loved her father more than she loved her own husband.

"Of course I do," she shouted back at him. "He was a *good* man—maybe the only good man. You will never be half the man my father—" That was when Carl lost control.

Hours later, Susanna regained consciousness. She reported her abusive spouse to the police for the first and the last time, then moved herself and Megan into a women's shelter. She'd never seen the locket since that awful night. Whether it had been lost in the scuffle or Carl had taken it was unclear. It had simply disappeared.

Tears were running down her cheeks now, and Susanna reached for the shelf unit to steady herself as she stared at the heart-shaped locket. Where had Matilda gotten this? How had she known? Furthermore, what did it mean? What was the point of experiencing such pain again?

"I see you found what you were looking for," Matilda said softly as she handed Susanna some tissues.

"What . . . ? How . . . ?" Susanna took the tissues and wiped her face, continuing to sob. She wondered if she'd ever be able to stop. Meanwhile Matilda just stood there, gently stroking Susanna's back, waiting for her to finish.

"Sometimes," Matilda began quietly, "hearts get broken, and being human, we try to fix them ourselves."

Susanna nodded. "That's true."

"Sometimes we think we protect our hearts . . . but we pile stone upon stone all the way around until we've built a sturdy wall."

With wide eyes, Susanna nodded again.

"We don't realize that a wall like that only *separates* us from what we need. It keeps us trapped inside . . . others trapped outside."

"Yes." Susanna took in a quick breath. "That's exactly right."

"Your daughter painted those words up there," Matilda said, pointing up to the wall over the front door. Susanna read the sentence, then tried to understand it.

> *New life, new hope, new joy will start*
> *when this is given from the heart.*

"When *what* is given from the heart?" Susanna asked.

"I think you know that answer."

"Love?"

Matilda just smiled.

Susanna looked down at the locket and sighed. Yes, it did make sense. She thought about Tommy and how she had put up her wall, pushing him away.

"Now the question is what are you going to do about it?" Matilda asked.

"Take down the wall?" Susanna said quietly.

Matilda nodded, then turned away and went back to the counter where the paperwork was still sitting. Susanna had no idea whether or not Matilda had read a single word of it. Part of her didn't care. She had no idea how she would explain this to anyone, but somehow the city needed to help keep this Christmas shop open.

Susanna went up to the counter and opened her purse, taking out her wallet. "How much do I owe you?"

Matilda laughed, waving her hand as if she didn't want Susanna's money. "Only putting that heart to good use."

"But I need to pay—"

Just then someone else entered the shop. "Thank you for shopping here today," Matilda told Susanna. "I'll be sure to look over those papers for you . . . when I have time. Now I need to see my customers."

Susanna didn't know what to do. As Matilda began to talk to a teen girl, Susanna felt like she should leave, give them some privacy. With the silver locket clutched in her hand, Susanna hurried out of the shop. Although she knew there was no reason to be embarrassed, she didn't want to be seen. Whatever had just happened—and she was certain that something had happened—she wanted to be alone to figure it all out. At least for the time being.

Helen knew that Tommy was troubled. Seriously troubled. She also knew there was nothing she could do about it. Whether he sold the newspaper and left town or stuck it out for one more Christmas season was up to him. Perhaps more than anyone in town, Helen understood Tommy. She knew how broken up he'd been to lose his father shortly after graduating college. Partly because it placed the family business on his reluctant shoulders. Partly because Tommy Sr. had passed on without resolving some issues with his sensitive son. And partly because it had all taken place during the holiday season.

Less than five years later, shortly after Tommy had fallen for Victoria, his mother was diagnosed with cancer. Tommy had been torn between his mother's illness, keeping the paper running, and making Victoria happy. He'd been planning to propose to Victoria on Christmas Eve, but then his mother had passed on just days before Christmas.

All along, Helen suspected that Victoria wasn't really in love with Tommy and would never marry him. She could see it in the pretty girl's eyes every time she came into the paper. Helen figured Victoria had been sticking around only out of pity, but it seemed heartless and cruel when she turned Tommy down on Christmas Eve, then left town just days later. It was no wonder Tommy hated the holidays.

Seeing him like this cut Helen to the core. Tommy was like a son to her. Even when she tried to be aloof—since he'd accused her of being too clingy one time—she always felt tuned in to his moods. If Tommy was sad, Helen was sad. She just wished there was some way to help him.

The more she'd thought about him during her visit in Florida, the more she'd wondered if being stuck with this newspaper was hurting him. Despite her loyalty to his parents, Helen hated to think that the family business had become Tommy's prison. Perhaps what he really needed was a fresh start. For that reason she was doing her best to appear impartial toward his decision, whichever way he went. However, unless she was wrong, her neutrality seemed to irk him even more.

She pondered these things as she watered the Boston fern by the front window, and just as she was pinching off a withered branch, she observed George Snider across the street. With his head down, he ducked into Matilda's shop. Knowing Councilman Snider and the way this debate over the Christmas Shoppe had heated up the past couple of weeks, she just knew that man was up to no good. Furthermore, she knew that Matilda did not deserve his wrath any more than she deserved the trash this town had been throwing her way lately.

Setting down the watering can with a clunk, Helen decided it was high time to do something about it. She intended to put a stop to the hostility right now! Without even getting her coat, Helen marched outside and looked both ways before she dashed across the street and into the shop. Just as she was getting ready to give that big oaf a piece of her mind, she saw a sight that nearly floored her. George was standing near the counter with both of Matilda's hands in his—and he was apologizing to her! His tone sounded genuine too. Helen could not believe her ears.

"I'm so sorry," he was telling Matilda. "I'll admit it took me awhile to figure things out. I know I've positioned myself as your worst enemy, but last night something happened. Something that changed me."

"Yes?" Matilda asked softly.

Helen desperately wanted to leave, but she felt trapped. Standing in the shadows of an aisle, she knew she would only draw attention to herself if she moved toward the door. And this seemed such a tender moment. Plus, she reminded herself, this was a public place. She would simply pretend to be doing some shopping.

"I was looking at that dad-burned piggy bank you made me take home," George continued. "Suddenly it all came rushing at me like a freight train. It just bowled me over, Matilda. Remember when you were talking about the truth the other day? I didn't get it then, but last night it was like a light went on inside my head. Suddenly I realized I'd been lying for years. My whole life has been nothing but a big fat lie." His voice choked slightly. "It all started back when I was just a kid. That time when I snuck money out of my piggy bank to buy candy and my father laid into me . . ."

Helen wanted to slip out as George continued to pour out

his heart, spilling a sad story of how his father would punish him and how that made George want to lie and steal all the more. How that made him feel guilty. How all his problems were related to money.

"Even though I don't actually steal anymore," he told Matilda, "I'm not an honest man. It's ruined a lot of good things, a lot of relationships. I think I'd like to change my ways, Matilda. I'd like to sleep well at night. I can't even remember the last time I slept all night."

Matilda pointed to a saying on the wall above the counter behind her. Helen, still standing in the shadows, looked up to read it too.

> *Sometimes so bright it's hard to see,*
> *this dear gift will set you free.*

"The truth is like that," Matilda gently told him. "Embrace the truth, George, and before long you will be sleeping like a baby."

They continued to talk as Helen inched her way toward the door, but just as she was reaching for the handle, someone else came rushing into the shop. Jed Thorpe, the owner of a cut-rate gas station on a backstreet—one of those sleazy places that people were always complaining about—came into the shop. With his head hanging nearly as low as his trousers, as if embarrassed to be seen in here, Jed shuffled toward the counter. Meanwhile, even as she stayed out of his way, Helen felt like her feet were glued to the floor.

She could tell George and Matilda were wrapping things up. As Matilda greeted Jed like a dear old friend, Helen made her escape. Rushing out the door, she realized that George was right on her heels. To her discomfort, he followed her to the edge of the sidewalk, where the wind was whipping right through her cashmere cardigan and silk blouse.

"Helen Fremont," he exclaimed. "How are you doing?"

"I'm just fine, George. Thank you." She wrapped her arms around herself for warmth as she waited for the traffic to clear.

"What were you doing in the Christmas Shoppe just now?" George asked in a tone that suggested he'd known she was there all along.

"I, uh, I was just doing some—"

"Did you hear what I told Matilda?"

Embarrassed, she just nodded as a delivery truck passed by.

To her surprise, George removed his overcoat and wrapped it around her shoulders. "Too cold to be out here without a wrap," he said. Acting like this was completely normal, he walked her across the street and into the newspaper building.

"Thank you." She smiled as she handed him back his coat, which was a nice London Fog with fleece lining. "That was very cavalier of you, George."

"You look surprised."

"Well . . . I . . . ." Helen pretended to busy herself by flipping through a pile of junk mail that she'd left on her desk and planned to take to the shredder.

"I'm thinking of turning over a new leaf," he said quietly. "I'm not sure how much you heard me say to Matilda just now."

"I didn't mean to eavesdrop, George, but I couldn't—"

"It's okay." He sat in the chair next to her desk, like he planned to stay awhile. "It was the oddest thing." He proceeded to tell her about a mysterious piggy bank Matilda had insisted on giving to him last week. "I know it sounds a bit strange," he said finally. "Even to me. Do you think I'm crazy?"

"No crazier than I am." Helen told him a bit about her own experience with the Tupperware measuring cups.

George blinked. "It's not just me?"

"Apparently not." Helen glanced back into the dimly lit building to see if anyone was around to overhear them—not that she cared too much—but as usual for a Friday afternoon, the place was deserted.

"I've decided that I'll do what I can to turn this thing around for Matilda and her Christmas shop," he said as he stood. "Time to do some damage control . . . see if I can undo some of the mess I've helped to make. I'm guessing my biggest challenge will be to convince the downtown merchants that she's no threat." He shook his head. "I'm sure they'll think I'm just as batty as she is."

"If you're batty, you're not the only one," she told him.

"Say, Helen . . ." He smiled warmly, revealing even white teeth. "Would you ever be interested in going to dinner with me?"

She tilted her head to one side. "You know, George, if you had asked me that same question yesterday, I would've politely declined."

He looked somewhat disappointed, then brightened. "But today?"

"Today I would say yes. I think I am interested."

"Can I call you this weekend?"

She nodded just as Tommy came in the front door. Probably

returning from the diner where he usually ate his lunch. George winked at Helen, then greeted Tommy.

"I read this week's editorial about Matilda Honeycutt's business," George informed Tommy in a semiserious tone.

"And?" Tommy peeled off his jacket and waited.

"If you'd asked me yesterday, I would've said, 'Good job, boy.'" George exchanged a knowing glance with Helen.

Tommy frowned. "And today?"

"Today I'd say you were pretty dang hard on the old girl. And I'd say it was mean-spirited on your part. Not a bit neighborly."

Tommy looked like he was about to topple over. "*What?*"

"Lighten up, boy," George said as he headed for the door. "Remember the kindliness of your parents back when they ran this paper, and don't forget it's Christmastime. Time for goodwill and peace on earth and all that warm fuzzy stuff." He tipped his head and made his exit.

Tommy turned and looked at Helen with a completely flummoxed expression. "I swear, Helen, this whole town is losing its mind!" He stormed off toward his office.

Helen considered following him and attempting to explain some things to him, but then she decided it might be wise to just let him cool off a bit first. Besides, it probably wouldn't hurt for him to think about these things. She'd already told him in no uncertain terms that she didn't agree with his editorial. She didn't like seeing Tommy turning into an old curmudgeon. Not at his age. It didn't look good on him.

Tommy was seriously questioning the general sanity of Parrish Springs right now. Maybe it was something in the water, or the air. Or maybe aliens had invaded, or else the entire town was possessed by some weird force. Oh, sure, he knew that was extreme, not to mention completely ridiculous. But people were acting very strange!

"I'm going home now," Helen announced as she poked her head into his office.

"I thought you'd already left." He peered up at her. "It *is* Friday, isn't it?"

"Yes, but I still had some catching up to do from last week. Any law against me working a whole day if I want to?"

"No, of course not."

"Besides," she reminded him, "if you sell this place, it might be smart to have things in order before you leave the country."

He just sighed and shook his head.

"Tommy," she began slowly, like she was weighing her words, "I know I already told you this, but I'm going to tell you again."

"What?"

"You should go and talk to Matilda Honeycutt."

"I tried," he said with some irritation. "I already told you that."

"I don't mean to interview or question her, Tommy. Just go over there and spend some time in her shop. Look around and—"

"And let her work her magic on me?" he teased.

"Call it what you will, but—"

"Come on, Helen, you don't believe in all that voodoo hoodoo, do you?" He chuckled at his cleverness. "Hey, that rhymes."

"I'm just asking you, Tommy, as your longtime friend." She gave him that look—that "I helped change your diapers" look. "As your good friend, I'm saying just go to her shop. But don't go with any judgment or agenda. Go with an open mind. Please. Just do it for me, Tommy. Consider it my Christmas present."

He rolled his eyes. "Oh, Helen."

"Don't 'oh, Helen' me, young man. Listen, you need—"

"Fine, fine." He waved his hand to stop her. "If it'll shut you up, I'll go. Okay?"

She brightened and stepped back. "Okay."

"By the way, what exactly was going on with you and our fine councilman when I walked in earlier? Looked like you two were having a nice little chat."

"If you really must know, George was asking me out."

Tommy laughed. "Hmm, let me guess, what did you tell the old goat?"

"I told the old goat yes."

Tommy almost fell out of his chair.

"People can change, Tommy." She put on her gloves.

"I guess."

She jingled her car keys like she was finished with this conversation. "Keep your promise to me, Tommy. Go to Matilda's and do some Christmas shopping!" She firmly closed his door.

"This town has gone mad!" He slammed his laptop closed. "Stark, raving mad." He looked at the clock. It was already past five. Matilda had probably closed her shop by now. But to appease Helen, he grabbed his jacket and things, turned off the lights in the building, and locked the door. He sauntered over to the Christmas Shoppe, hoping that despite the OPEN sign, it would actually be closed. Since the door was unlocked, he went inside.

Sounds of West Coast jazz music floated through the air, the very thing his parents used to listen to when he was a kid, and for some reason it was comforting to hear it today. It reminded him of better days.

He had no idea what he was doing here, except that he'd promised Helen. He browsed the strangely filled shelves, wondering who on earth could want any of this junk. Seriously, there was a lot better stuff in his parents' attic—which reminded him he'd have to deal with all that if he sold their house and left Parrish Springs to journey around the world.

He gazed blankly at a broken leather dog collar, a pair of old golf shoes, and a child-sized tea set that was chipped and missing pieces. Then he stopped. He picked up a snow globe and just stared at it in wonder. Something about it was so familiar. There was no water inside and the glass globe was cloudy from time, but when he peered closely, putting his eye right next to the clearest spot, he spied the nativity scene inside. The same tiny donkey and cow and sheep that he remembered, and the holy family of three inside the little brown stable. Still safe and sound. Well, except for the missing water and snow.

Tommy felt a lump in his throat as he stared at the object in his hands. A bittersweet feeling washed over him as he remembered two very specific incidents related to that exact same snow globe. The first one was sweet . . .

Tommy was seven and still believed in Santa Claus when his mother presented him with the snow globe a couple of weeks before Christmas. "I want you to always remember what the real Christmas is about," she'd told him one evening as he enjoyed shaking the globe to make the snow fall all over the animals and family. Then she told him about how God had sent the best Christmas present ever in the form of a tiny baby.

"How can a *baby* be a present?" Tommy asked with little-boy skepticism.

"Because that particular baby was God's very own Son, and he grew up into a man who saved the world."

"Like Superman?" Tommy said with enthusiasm.

"Sort of," she said. "Only better. Jesus came to earth so that we could be *friends* with God."

Tommy tried to imagine that. "We can be friends with God?"

"That's right," she assured him. "Jesus died to show how much God loves us."

"Jesus died?" Tommy gasped.

"Then Jesus came back to life," she said quickly, "so when

159

we die, we get to live with Jesus and God in their beautiful kingdom forever."

"Oh . . ." Tommy thought he sort of got it. Back then anyway. Back then the snow globe held meaning and sweetness and hope.

But time passed and Christmases came and went. Tommy had packed the snow globe away after his father died . . . shortly before Christmas. Then not too many years later his mother died . . . shortly before Christmas. And then Victoria dumped him . . . on Christmas Eve. That's when Tommy decided he was sick of Christmas, that he didn't believe in Christmas. Later when he'd found the snow globe wrapped in tissue paper, packed in a box, he'd carefully removed it and then thrown that blasted thing into the fireplace. He'd watched the glass shatter and heard the water sputter in the flames. And that had been the end of it.

He stared at the old snow globe in his hands. The glass seemed even cloudier now, but he realized that was only because his eyes were brimming with tears. That surprised him, because he'd been certain that he, like the snow globe, had been emptied long, long ago. But standing there in the Christmas Shoppe, Tommy let his tears flow freely down his face, with the soft strains of jazz music playing in the background.

He had no idea how long he stood there, or even what was going on inside of him, but finally he realized it was probably getting late. Surely Matilda would like to close up her shop, although he hadn't seen her about anywhere. He looked around, calling out her name and suddenly feeling very guilty for the way he'd treated her, the way he'd misjudged her, scorned her in his bitter editorial. Of course she would be avoiding him. Why would she want to speak to someone like him?

"Hello," he called up the stairs. "Matilda?"

"I'm over here," she called as she emerged from the back room.

"I'm sorry to disturb you," he said, "but I'd like to purchase this."

She smiled. "I see you found what you needed."

He nodded. "First I'd like to apologize to you. Did you see this week's newspaper?"

She shook her head.

"Well, no matter. I'm still sorry about what I wrote. I clearly did not understand you. I hope you can forgive me."

She smiled. "Of course. You know that I do."

He sighed. Somehow he did know that. Deep inside of him, he knew.

"So are you all ready for Christmas this year?" she asked, sounding almost like a normal shop owner.

"Yes . . . I think I am. I'm getting there anyway." He held up the snow globe. "How much do I owe you for this?"

She waved her hand. "It's yours, Tommy."

"No, but I want to pay—"

"Please, don't insult me. It's yours. You know it is."

He felt the lump in his throat returning as he nodded. "Yes," he murmured. "I know it is." He stepped away. "Thank you, Matilda," he said gruffly. "Thank you so much!" Feeling almost like he was seven years old again, Tommy turned and hurried out onto the street, where snowflakes were starting to fly.

It wasn't until the next morning that Tommy felt emotionally ready to have an actual conversation with anyone. He decided to start with Helen. Instead of calling her, he walked over to her house. About an inch of snow had fallen last night, and the sound of it crunching under his boots reminded him of being a boy. So much reminded him of being a boy.

"What are you doing here?" Helen asked as he came up the walk she had just started shoveling.

"Merry Christmas, Helen!" He took the shovel from her, then hugged her.

"What?" she cried as she stepped back and stared at him.

"I kept my promise to you," he told her as he began to shovel her walk.

"You went to the Christmas Shoppe!"

"I did." He grinned at her and tossed a shovelful of snow into her yard.

"And something happened?"

"I think I get it," he said as he pushed the shovel. "I

understand the real meaning of Christmas now. Just like my mom told me so long ago."

"You do?" Helen's eyes grew wide. "Perhaps you can explain it to me then."

He laughed. "Oh, surely you already know."

"Maybe." She tilted her head to one side. "Maybe not."

"Well, I'll be happy to tell you what I know." He finished up the last shovelful. "But first I need to pay a visit to the city manager."

She blinked. "The city manager?"

"Susanna Elton."

Her eyes got a knowing look. "Oh?"

"I need to apologize to her."

"I see . . ." Helen looked extremely curious.

"Yes, I will tell you the whole story later. Okay?"

She grinned as he handed her back the shovel. "Okay!"

"See you around, Helen," he called as he continued down the street toward Susanna's house, where the walk had already been shoveled.

"Hey, Tommy, look out," Megan called as she threw a snowball at him.

He laughed, then gathered up some snow, formed a ball, and tossed it back. "What do you think of this snow?"

"I love it!" she said as she came over. Her cheeks were rosy and her dark eyes shining. "We never got snow like this back where we used to live."

"Is your mom home?" he asked.

"Yeah, but I thought you were mad at her."

He smiled sheepishly. "I was never mad at her, Megan. I just wasn't thinking straight."

"And now you are?" Megan led him to the front porch.

"I sure am."

She opened the door, calling into the house, "Hey, Mom! Someone here to see you!" She turned and grinned at him. "I'd go inside with you, but my friend Shelby is on her way over here. We're going to make a snow horse."

"A snow horse?"

She shrugged. "Well, we're going to try."

"Hello?" he called as he went inside, taking off his boots so as not to track snow into the house. "Susanna?"

She came around the corner looking even more beautiful than he remembered. Her long, dark hair hung loose on her shoulders, and she had on a sweater and jeans. She looked curiously at him, and suddenly Tommy felt totally out of place and very self-conscious. Really, what was he thinking dropping in on her like this? Who did he think he was anyway?

"Uh, sorry to intrude like this," he said quickly, "but I just wanted to come over and tell you that I'm sorry. I'm really, really sorry, Susanna."

She looked surprised. "Sorry? For what?"

He began to explain, briefly at first, but as she encouraged him, he poured out more of the story, even telling her about the snow globe and the real meaning of Christmas. "I know," he said finally, "I probably sound crazy. To be honest, just yesterday I thought everyone in town was losing their minds. Or at least some of them. And now . . . does any of this make any sense?"

She smiled. "Total sense." She tugged a black ribbon from the neck of her sweater. A heart-shaped silver locket was attached, and she proceeded to tell him about her own experience at the Christmas Shoppe. "I've had a wall around my heart for years now, Tommy," she said. "It's coming down now."

He just looked at her, longing to hold on to this moment.

"Are you still planning to sell the newspaper?" she asked softly.

"No," he assured her. "I've decided against that."

"Really?" Her eyes lit up. "You'll be sticking around then?"

"Oh yes." He nodded. "I'll definitely be sticking around."

"Thanks to Matilda's shop?"

"Yes. And that brings me to something else. I want to do something to help Matilda . . . perhaps make up for that nasty editorial I wrote last week."

"That was bad."

"I know. I already apologized, but that's not enough. I already began a new editorial to tell the rest of the story, but it won't be out until Wednesday. From what I hear, the city might be putting her out of business by then."

Susanna frowned. "I just don't see any other way around it, Tommy. I tried to talk her into letting me get her an exemption. Even the mayor wants to help her. But it's like she doesn't want our help."

"I know. Yet she's helping everyone. I was thinking about that this morning, and I got an idea."

"An idea?"

"Yes. I could be wrong, but I have a feeling that no money has been exchanged in her shop."

Susanna's eyes lit up. "She wouldn't let me pay for my locket!"

"She wouldn't take money from me either," he said. "Helen said the same thing about her experience, and I know George Snider received his gift for free."

"So if there's no money involved—if she's giving everything away—then there is no need for a business permit . . . of any kind." Susanna grinned. "You know what that means?"

"No one can drive a business out of business if it's not really a business?"

"Absolutely."

"Should we go tell Matilda?"

"Why not."

Tommy felt like a kid as he and Susanna walked through the snow toward town. The sun came out and everything looked charmingly sweet, just like an old Christmas card, as they strolled through the downtown district.

"I'll let you tell her," Tommy said as he opened the door for Susanna, "since you're the city manager."

"Thank you!" She smiled at him.

"And I'll write the article about it."

Together they went to the counter. Matilda had on a long purple velvet dress today—straight out of the sixties. With the feather duster in her hand poised like a scepter, Tommy thought she almost looked like a shabby sort of queen. Queen of the thrift shop.

"Hello, dears," she said warmly.

"Good morning, Matilda," Tommy said.

"I'm so happy to see you two together." Matilda came around from behind the counter.

"And we're so happy to see you," Susanna said. She proceeded to tell Matilda the good news.

166

"Oh, that's nice." Matilda nodded as she dusted a shelf. Susanna exchanged a glance with Tommy.

"Anyway, we just wanted you to know," he told her.

"I appreciate that." She smiled at both of them just as someone entered the shop. "If you'll excuse me, I have a customer to see to."

They told her goodbye and exited the shop.

"She didn't seem too excited about the good news," Susanna said with a tinge of disappointment in her voice.

"I think it's because she'd never been concerned in the first place," Tommy said as they walked down the sidewalk. "It's like she's always been okay about everything."

"That's true. Like she had the confidence that it would all work out."

"Seems like she was right too." Tommy sighed. "It's all working out."

When they came to the crosswalk, Susanna reached for his hand. "Do you mind?" she asked a bit shyly.

He chuckled. "Not at all. I think it's a very safe practice to hold hands while crossing the street." To his relief, she continued to hold his hand all the way back to her house. He had a feeling that this was only the beginning of a whole lot of hand-holding to look forward to in the future.

No one in Parrish Springs could recall exactly when Matilda Honeycutt left town. Some said it was before Christmas. Some said it was afterward. But most of them agreed on one thing—Parrish Springs was never the same after her visit.

It wasn't until January that the town discovered that

Councilman Snider had secretly purchased the Barton Building from Matilda shortly before her hasty departure. No one knew the exact price, but no one seemed to care, since instead of allowing a discount store to occupy that space, George and his new girlfriend, Helen Fremont, planned to open a new gift shop. They would keep the old sign that Matilda had put up, and the theme would continue to be Christmas, only now the shop would sell new merchandise, or mostly . . .

Of course, George and Helen's relationship wasn't the only new romance to develop during the holidays. Word spread fast that the new city manager and the old confirmed bachelor and owner of the *Spout* had gotten engaged on New Year's Eve. Yes, it was starting out to be a very fine year in Parrish Springs. No telling what might happen by next Christmas!

Melody Carlson is the prolific author of more than two hundred books, including fiction, nonfiction, and gift books for adults, young adults, and children. She is also the author of *Three Days*, *The Gift of Christmas Present*, *The Christmas Bus*, *An Irish Christmas*, *All I Have to Give*, *The Christmas Dog*, and *Christmas at Harrington's*. Her writing has won several awards, including a Gold Medallion for *King of the Stable* (Crossway, 1998) and a Romance Writers of America Rita Award for *Homeward* (Multnomah, 1997). She lives with her husband in Sisters, Oregon. Visit her website at www.melodycarlson.com.

A Note from the Editors

We hope you enjoy *The Christmas Shoppe* by Melody Carlson, specially selected by the editors of the Books and Inspirational Media Division of Guideposts, a nonprofit organization that touches millions of lives every day through products and services that inspire, encourage, help you grow in your faith, and celebrate God's love in every aspect of your daily life.

Thank you for making a difference with your purchase of this book, which helps fund our many outreach programs to military personnel, prisons, hospitals, nursing homes, and educational institutions. To learn more, visit GuidepostsFoundation.org.

We also maintain many useful and uplifting online resources. Visit Guideposts.org to read true stories of hope and inspiration, access OurPrayer network, sign up for free newsletters, download free e-books, join our Facebook community, and follow our stimulating blogs.

To learn about other Guideposts publications, including the best-selling devotional *Daily Guideposts*, go to ShopGuideposts.org, call (800) 932-2145, or write to Guideposts, PO Box 5815, Harlan, Iowa 51593.

Sign up for the
Guideposts Fiction Newsletter
and stay up-to-date on
the fiction you love!

You'll get sneak peeks of new releases, recommendations from other Guideposts readers, and special offers just for you . . .

And it's FREE!

**Just go to Guideposts.org/newsletters
today to sign up.**

**Visit ShopGuideposts.org
or call (800) 932-2145**

Find more inspiring fiction in these best-loved Guideposts series

Secrets of the Blue Hill Library
Enjoy the tingle of suspense and the joy of coming home when Anne Gibson turns her late aunt's Victorian mansion into a library and uncovers hidden secrets.

Miracles of Marble Cove
Follow four women who are drawn together to face life's challenges, support one another in faith, and experience God's amazing grace as they encounter mysterious events in the small town of Marble Cove.

Secrets of Mary's Bookshop
Delve into a cozy mystery where Mary, the owner of Mary's Mystery Bookshop, finds herself using sleuthing skills that she didn't realize she had. There are quirky characters and lots of unexpected twists and turns.

Patchwork Mysteries
Discover that life's little mysteries often have a common thread in a series where every novel contains an intriguing mystery centered around a quilt located in a beautiful New England town.

Mysteries of Silver Peak
Escape to the historic mining town of Silver Peak, Colorado, and discover how one woman's love of antiques helps her solve mysteries buried deep in the town's checkered past.

**To learn more about these books,
visit ShopGuideposts.org**